ENCHANTED GODS

CURSED

USA TODAY BESTSELLING AUTHOR

K.K. ALLEN

ENCHANTED GODS

CURSED

USA TODAY BESTSELLING AUTHOR

K.K. ALLEN

COPYRIGHT

Copyright © 2021 by K.K. Allen
Cover Design: Emily Wittig Designs
Editing / Proofreading: Red Adept Editing

Contact SayHello@KK-Allen.com with questions.

ISBN: 9798527935509

For my son, Jagger. Your Enchanted spirit inspires me every single day. Never stop dreaming. I love you.

PROLOGUE

As the wind swirls, fueling the raging fire at my back, I now know her words to be true. *What makes us most powerful can also kill us.*

I'm Earth's prisoner, sinking deeper into the sand and watching helplessly as a growing wave closes in on me until its massive form towers over the shore.

Fire, water, earth, and air. It was all supposed to be in my control. Something went terribly wrong.

They told me to stay away, that love was a dangerous game to play. I didn't listen. And now I'm paying the ultimate price.

I take one final glance in his direction, my heart aching as I say a silent goodbye. It's time to let fate take its natural course.

The wave folds over and crashes on me, the force of it releasing me from the sand's grip then sweeping me off my feet. Its currents throw me like a rag doll, ripping me far from shore. With all my strength and remaining breath, I claw my way to the surface. I don't know how far I need to rise, so I just keep fighting while my throat burns from lack of oxygen. The current is as resilient as an anchor.

I've lost all air, and I can feel myself grow weaker until all I see is black. Unable to hold on to my power any longer, I release my will and float free within the quieting water, slowly overcome by an eerie peace.

Not even my magic can save me now.

ONE

My dirt-covered sneakers kick beneath me like a pendulum, timed perfectly with the beating of my heart. *Tick. Tick. Tick.* As if that isn't already a haunting soundtrack to my thoughts, the second hand on the clock above my head grows louder, providing more chaos to my already-cluttered mind.

The waiting game is longer today than normal. That's fitting, considering the hard glare my mom gave me before strolling straight past me and through the door to my principal's office. I try to combat the visual of my mom's anger and the guilt that comes with it by searching my thoughts for something else—anything else. It's close to impossible. The only other image flashing through my mind is of that cocky jock Steve Salmon and the crude words he muttered to me right before he went crashing through the first-story window of our science class.

"I'm so sorry about this, Erica. I thought therapy was helping her deal with her anger issues." My mom's voice is faint through the walls but clear enough for me to make out every word.

"Oh, Grace," Principal Waverly says sympathetically, because apparently they're on a first-name basis. "I know you're doing everything you can. Maybe homeschool will be a better option for her. Then she can continue to get the extra help while keeping up with her schoolwork. She's a great student. If it wasn't for these little outbursts, she'd be thriving and well on her way to an Ivy League school after graduation. I just can't put our students at risk any longer."

"So what does this mean for Katrina? There's only a month left of school. What about graduation?"

"I'm afraid it means Kat will be expelled from Silver Lake High, pending an expulsion hearing. However, if you choose to take her out willingly to homeschool, then we can forego the formal process. Then she'll still have a chance to graduate on time. However, she will not be invited to the ceremony to walk along with her peers. I'm so sorry."

I bow my head, feelings of shame and disappointment snaking through me. Principal Waverly has always been kind to me. Understanding to a fault. But not even she can save me this time. No one wants me here.

My mom starts to cry. "I don't know how it got so bad."

The sound of a tissue sliding from the rectangular box at the edge of Principal Waverly's desk paints a sad image in my mind. It seems like all I've been doing lately is making my mom cry.

"Kat needs to understand what's bothering her deep inside so she can better control her actions. Maybe this has something to do with her father. Have you been in touch with him?"

"No." My mom snaps the word. "Not since Katrina was

born. But he's not the problem. She doesn't even ask about him."

The silence that follows is heavy enough to weigh down my heart.

"Well, she's got to be curious at least—"

"She's not."

The sound of a chair scraping the floor tells me their conversation is over, which doesn't surprise me. There are many reasons why I don't ask about my father, my mother's coldness toward the subject being one of them. I tune out the remaining chitchat and instead focus on how I'm going to face my mom after this "incident," as everyone calls it.

A few minutes later, the door to Principal Waverly's office opens, and my mom steps out, her eyes red and still moist from crying. She locks those sad eyes with mine and holds out her hand to me. "Let's go home and have a chat."

I look from her to the principal before frowning. "I didn't push Steve. I barely even touched him."

Principal Waverly gives me a small smile before placing a hand on my shoulder. "I believe you had no intention of hurting Steve, but there are too many witnesses who saw things differently. It's important for you to take responsibility for your actions."

Her words aren't cold in the least, but it still feels like a hard slap in the face. No one wants to hear me out. No one will even consider that there's another side to the story. It hurts. My chest squeezes. Defeated, I finally take my mom's hand.

She says nothing as we walk to my locker, then she tells me to empty it. There's not much to pack up. My course books, a light green jacket I haven't worn since early spring, and a hanging mirror I used more for looking out for sneak attacks from my classmates than I ever used it to check my own reflection.

I've just gathered the last of my things when the bell rings, signaling the end of class. I freeze, and I can see in my mom's eyes that she's dreading what comes next too.

She leans in to whisper, "Keep your head straight forward and don't react. Got it?"

I nod and squeeze my lids together, summoning the courage I know I'll need. Then we walk toward the entrance. The heckling begins as soon as everyone begins to pour into the halls.

"Look. There she is. Did you see what she did to Steve?"

"No, but I heard about it. Katrina Summer is a freak."

"Well, I was there. It was terrifying. I hope his parents sue."

"I doubt they will. He doesn't have a scratch on him. How is that even possible?"

"Who knows? But Kat's a fucking psycho. I'm glad she's leaving."

"Look at what she's carrying. Hopefully, she's gone for good this time."

"She's so tragic. I mean, look at that dress. She must have the same one in fifty different shades."

I swallow over the lump in my throat as my mom pushes open the front door for me to exit first. She leads me to a set of bikes parked on the rack. My mom has never driven, so we walk or ride our bikes everywhere we go.

I assume we're riding directly to our apartment, but we

take a detour to the outdoor ice cream stand instead. It's always been my favorite, with the top of its small roof shaped like a pink swirl of ice cream covered with rainbow glitter, but it's not usually a stop we make when I've done something bad at school.

"Mom—" I start, but she shakes her head to cut me off.

"This stop isn't for you. It's for me."

I snap my mouth closed and step back while she orders two strawberry milkshakes. We sit down at a blue table with a matching blue umbrella. I try to enjoy the creamy sweetness sliding down the back of my throat, but it's impossible with our future conversation looming over my head.

"I didn't push him." I can't hold back the tears anymore. "I barely touched him. I only put my hands on him because he touched me first."

"That boy put his hands on you?"

I can see the fury in my mother's eyes. "Yes. After he told the entire school that I slept with him. I've never even seen Steve outside of school. And I haven't—"

"Katrina." She sighs. "I believe you. I do. And if what you're saying is true, then maybe Steve deserved to fly out a window, but I'm not worried about that boy right now. I'm worried about *you*. You have got to learn how to control your anger." She takes my hand and squeezes it. "I don't think you know your own strength at times, and that's not something the school can consider as an excuse. That's why I'm pulling you from Silver Lake High and enrolling you in online courses. You only have another month until the end of the year, and then you'll be at the community college. Your best bet to get into a four-year institution is to keep a low profile, and we'll get you some help in the meantime."

College. The dreaded subject. My mom has insisted on me furthering my education since I was a little girl. I don't understand the point of it. And with how broke we always seem to be, I can't imagine even being able to go when it's time. But I don't argue with her about it because I know how much it means to her. If anything, I try to avoid the subject.

"What if nothing helps me? It's like I'm cursed. What if bad things just happen when I'm around?"

She averts her eyes and shakes her head. "You are not cursed. And no, bad things don't just happen when you're around. You just..." She clamps her mouth shut without finishing her thought, then she turns back to me and tilts her head. "I'm going to help you live a normal life."

A chill snakes through me at her words. *A normal life?* What does that even mean?

"There's something I want to give you."

My mom begins to fiddle with the gold charm bracelet that wraps her wrist. It holds a single heart-shaped locket, and she's worn it for as long as I can remember. She always seems to be touching it in some way, but she does something I've never seen her do before—she unclasps it. Her breath is sharp, and her eyes close when the jewelry slides away from her skin. After a brief pause, she slips it around my wrist, her hands shaking.

"Do you remember the story about how I met your father?"

I swallow, feeling panicked as I search her eyes. If she's bringing up my father, she must be trying to tell me something important. "You met him in Apollo Beach after you washed ashore. He carried you into his parents' home, and you fell in love."

My mom nods slowly then reaches out to touch the locket hanging from my wrist. "This was the only item I carried with me. Like my life before Apollo Beach, I don't know how I got it or where it came from. Yet strangely, I know it's protected me over the years. Just like I know it will protect you."

I stare at the beautiful chain, a sick feeling swirling in my stomach. I've always sensed a deeper story to my mom's past that she's never been willing to tell me. "What do we need protection from?"

My mom just shrugs and gives me a soft smile. "Ourselves. Promise me you'll never take it off, no matter what."

I blink back at her, wondering if she's serious.

"Promise me, Katrina."

Hearing the sharpness in her tone, I nod. "I promise."

"Good." She moves to my bench, wraps an arm around my shoulders, and presses a kiss to my temple. "Let this charm remind you of all the good you possess. And please," she adds with a laugh, "put some other charms on it while you're at it."

I promise her that I will and follow her lead to drop the conversation. She smiles while we finish our milkshakes and begin debating which movie to watch tonight. My mom always suggests thought-provoking dramas like *Memento* and *Gone Girl*, while I aim for romantic comedies like *10 Things I Hate About You* and *Clueless*.

By the time we park our bikes and walk up the two

flights of stairs to our third-story apartment, we've narrowed it down to two options.

"Let me hear your pitch," she challenges as she sticks her key in the door. "Why should we watch *The Butterfly Effect?*"

"You first." I fold my arms across my chest. "Why should we watch *Eternal Sunshine of the Spotless Mind?*"

There's a grin on my mom's face when she pushes open the door, and I almost forget the terrible portion of the day that came before now. She's just opened her mouth to respond when her pocket buzzes, alerting her of a new message.

"Damn," my mom says, her eyes on her cell phone screen. "I have to go back to work."

I didn't think my day could get any worse. "No. You're kidding me, right? It's your night off."

She sighs and reaches for her purse. "I know, but I had to leave in a hurry to get to the school. A patient needs discharge papers. I'm just going to run to work, type up my notes, and then I'll be back here in time to start the movie. Two hours, tops."

I groan and roll my eyes. "Fine. I'll take a bath or something."

My mom's eyes light up. "Great idea, sweetheart. Take a bath. Read a book soon. I'll be back." She leans over and kisses the top of my head. "I love you, Katrina."

"Love you, too, Mom."

DARKNESS, emptiness, loss. I'm swimming through the fiery depths of my own thoughts—past, present, and future—when I'm ripped from my slumber by three hard knocks on the front door. My mind is trapped in a fog, but I can feel my body aching from my having fallen asleep on our tattered, stiff green couch. I yawn and look at the digital clock above the television. It's three in the morning. The television is on, but it's stuck on the menu screen from the movie I started streaming earlier, and the bowl of popcorn I made hours ago is still sitting half-full on the coffee table. I must have passed out early.

Knock. Knock. Knock.

"Mom?" I stand up and scan the apartment.

I check her room. Her bed is still made. I look in the bathroom. No sign of her. Finally, I walk toward the front entrance and discover that her purse and keys are missing from the table near the front door, where she normally places them. She should have been home hours ago.

It's times like this I wish my mom wasn't so against simple methods of communication like cell phones and email. She's always warned me away from the addictive technology that will consume my life if I'm not careful. I swear she would have put me in homeschool sooner if she didn't have to work so much.

Another round of knocks pound at the door, making me jump. I take another step to reach the door and peek through the little hole. The moment I see the police uniform, my entire body freezes. I can feel the blood draining from my face and pumping through my veins. Everything is racing—my heart, my mind. I can't shake the dark, awful thoughts I've been experiencing lately. It feels like everything that's happened over the past two years has escalated into this pivotal point, but I don't know why. I don't know what any of it means, but I can't avoid whatever this is any longer.

I unlock the door, pull it open, and face the two uniformed men, who have unmistakable sorrow in their eyes.

"Hello, Miss. We're looking for Katrina Summer, daughter of Grace Summer. Is that you?"

I nod slowly, as if that simple act will delay the inevitable. I look down at my wrist where my mom's bracelet now rests, and somehow, I already know what they're about to tell me.

TWO

I 'll never forget that hollow, rhythmic pounding on the door or the expressions on the officers' faces as they delivered the news.

"We regret to inform you that your mother was in an unfortunate accident."

I insisted that they'd made a mistake, that they had the wrong apartment. My mother was still at work. Then they described her blue vintage bicycle, including the tattered brown seat and large woven basket. That was all it took for my entire world to turn black.

I've existed in a numb state for the past few days. It's like I'm living outside my body, hovering and watching the aftermath of my mother's death unfold like one big horrible nightmare. I wish it was only a nightmare. I'm no stranger to those. But I know I'll never be able to shake this dark reality, not even if they do find the person responsible for ending my mother's life. Justice isn't enough to replace what I lost.

If I hadn't gotten into trouble at school, she would never have had to go back to work in the first place. And then maybe she wouldn't have taken off the bracelet that, in her mind, protected her all these years. If it weren't for me, she would still be here. I can't turn back the clock, and that fact alone creates an all-consuming guilt that I'll live with forever.

"We're almost there, Katrina. Just a few more minutes."

The blond woman driving introduced herself to me at the police station as my grandmother's caretaker, Charlotte. She seems nice enough, but the fact that everyone expected for me to get up and leave with her as if we were old friends was the most unnerving experience. From there, she made sure the police had the information they needed from me, helped me gather my things, and arranged for a moving company to take the rest of our belongings and apartment furnishings to a storage facility. Now, we're on our way to my grandmother's home in Florida.

I tug at the chain wrapped around my wrist. My skin is rubbed raw beneath it. The damn piece of jewelry feels like more of a handcuff than a present from my mother. The stubborn latch refuses to open, and no matter what I try to snap the chain, it won't come off. With a frustrated sigh, I release the bracelet and pinch my lids closed.

The drive from Silver Lake to Apollo Beach is over nine hours, but it feels as if we've been moving through quicksand, the earth is swallowing me whole as the world I once knew slowly disappears from view. A chill sweeps over me as I take in the unfamiliar setting. There is an immediate sense of distinction and exclusivity in the coastal city just south of Tampa.

We turn onto a main drive and slow as we pass dozens of residential inlets. Squinting, I struggle to make out smokestacks in the near distance, their white plumes evaporating into the darkening sky. It's such a strange sight compared to the spacious and immaculate appearance of the rest of the town. Every building we drive by looks brand-new, and every car we pass appears to sparkle like it just came from the wash. Even in the fading sunlight, I can see that the landscape is perfectly fitting for a home-and-garden magazine.

"Once you settle in, I think you'll love it here." Charlotte tosses me a small, tentative smile. "We live in a small town, but I assure you, it's a lively one. You'll make friends in no time and..."

My gaze catches on the T in the road ahead as I tune Charlotte out. She's been nothing but nice to me since the moment I met her, but I'm in no mood for awkward small talk. Instead, I focus on a guy jogging on the sidewalk in front of us. Even from here, I can see that he's muscular and fit, like a pro-wrestler ready for the fight of his life. He's wearing a black cap that shades his eyes, a black tank top that grips his muscles in all the right places, and a pair of black shorts that hang down to his knees.

I'm transfixed by his perfect technique—steady and effortless. It's a strange thing to notice, but I love the sport of running. It has been the only form of a healthy release that has worked for me over the past two years. Even though I made a daily habit of putting in the miles, I was never good enough to make Silver Lake High's team. But this guy...

I'm caught up in his rhythm, finding his pacing almost soothing to my soul, when he grips the bottom of his top and yanks it over his head, revealing a sheen of sweat on deliciously taut muscles. My heart jumps into my throat. They don't make boys like him in Silver Lake—I know that much.

We're approaching the T in the road just as he starts to jog across our path. He's close enough that I can maybe see his eyes beneath the shade of his cap, so I try. I don't know why my curiosity about this guy is at an all-time high, but I can't stop wishing he would just look up. Just once, so I can see him.

Charlotte turns left so the guy is directly to my right. *Look up,* my thoughts command as if he can hear me.

He slows, his chin tips up, and his shaded gaze finds mine. A current of energy zaps me and runs through my veins like I've been lit from within. He stops in his tracks, his bare chest heaving and revealing his exertion, and he turns his head to hold my stare.

For a split second, I imagine he feels it, too—a connection, a spark, something—but his gaze darkens into a full-blown glare, filling me with pure and utter mortification. He might as well have dumped a bucket of ice water over my head. The aftershock is worse than the initial sting.

My embarrassment is slowly seeping through my clothes and my pores until it shocks me to the bone, jolting me right back to the present.

I gasp and look forward before blinking hard and sliding down farther into my seat. *What the hell was that?*

"Katrina, are you okay?"

I turn to face Charlotte, knowing that the rapid rise and fall of my chest is a dead giveaway to my nerves. At least she doesn't know what caused my reaction. That would be humiliating. I just got caught ogling some grumpy-looking dude who was out for an innocent run. "Yeah. I-I'm fine." I shake my head and bite down on my bottom lip, knowing my words are a lie. I'm not fine at all. "You said we're almost there?"

Her smile reaches her eyes, calming me some, then she looks forward and nods, gesturing to something. I look out the front windshield to find a large wrought-iron gate with a gold *S* ornament at its center and a security booth between two lanes of traffic. Charlotte stops to activate the gate. A sign just in front of the guard booth that reads Summer Estates.

I furrow my brows at the irony. "*Summer* Estates? As in Rose Summer, my grandmother, or is that a coincidence?"

Charlotte's brightening smile answers my question before she speaks. "It's no coincidence, Katrina. Your grandparents funded the development of this neighborhood nearly forty years ago." She does a double take, her smile slipping some. "How much has your mom told you about Apollo Beach and your grandmother?"

I wonder if my expression is as blank as my knowledge. "Nothing, really. Just that Rose lives here and that things were complicated between the two of them."

Charlotte nods and rests her shoulders back against the seat. "Well, then I suppose there is a lot of catching up to do."

I cringe at the thought of catching up with a family member who hasn't tried at all to get to know me. I'm dreading every bit of my new situation, but I know better than to act on my thoughts. My mother's death shocked us all. I should be grateful that my grandmother offered to take me in, but that feeling is lost beneath the grief that still rocks my soul.

We enter the subdivision, if one can even call it that. Houses the size of museums sit on either side of the winding street, complete with marble drives, intricate stone carvings, and large columns. The three-decades-old community appears to be in immaculate condition. My stomach turns as discomfort snakes through me. I do not belong here.

We pull into the rounded drive at the back corner of the street, where the biggest house of them all looms before us. My jaw drops, and I look at Charlotte, waiting for her to start laughing and tell me that this is all one big joke. This cannot be my grandmother's home. Amusement is not what I find on her face.

"Welcome to Summer Manor, Katrina." Charlotte beams. "You're home."

I register that word again with a shudder. It rattles me now more than when she said it earlier. *Home.* This is not my home.

I vaguely remember my mom mentioning something of my grandmother's wealth, but this is not what I pictured.

"I didn't realize..." The sight of the towering Greek-structured villa before me silences me.

"Katrina?"

The formality of Charlotte enunciating my name snaps me out of my trance, and I examine her for the first time since meeting her. She is beautiful—around my mother's age, I think—with a nice figure, flawless skin, perfect hair, and shining light-blue eyes.

I pinch out the best smile I can muster under the circumstances. She really has been kind to me. "You can call me Kat, you know. No one really calls me by my full name."

Charlotte nods, showing she is all too willing to oblige. "Of course. Kat, it is." She smiles and turns off the car. "Leave your things. I'll have them brought up shortly."

I step out of the car. The peaceful sound of a water fountain comes from the base of the steps, where a rock marble statue of Apollo and Daphne stands at its center. My breath catches in my throat at the beautifully depicted moment in time when Apollo catches up to the river god's daughter and she transforms into a laurel tree.

Greek mythology was the only part of English class that intrigued me, and I remember their story vividly. A revengeful Eros fired one gold-tipped arrow at Apollo, making him fall helplessly in love with Daphne. Eros then fired a lead-tipped arrow at Daphne, making her impervious to Apollo's love and indifferent to his advances. When Apollo pursued her, Daphne ran to her father, Peneus, and begged for his help. He obliged, using metamorphosis to transform her.

Everything about the statue brings the entire story to life in one glimpse. The way Apollo's arm circles Daphne's torso, yet touches nothing save for the bark of the laurel tree that's sprouting between them. The way bark grows above the earth and forms around her, with her fingers morphing into branches that have leaves sprouting from them, all while her toes transform into roots. Even their arched bodies, flowing drapery, and facial expressions reveal Apollo's surprise and Daphne's horror in a moment frozen in time. It's the most beautiful piece of artwork I think I've ever seen.

Breaking out of my trance, I follow Charlotte up the rounded marble steps, taking each one carefully as if not to disturb the stone at my feet. The home in front of me—or I should say *mansion?*—is bigger than the entire three-story apartment complex I lived in with my mom. Am I seriously going to live here?

All the while, Charlotte sounds like a tour director reading from cue cards, personalized for my arrival. She talks about a rock pier and a private beach where neighbors gather for festivities. I listen passively as I follow her up to the front doors. I expected something nice and luxurious, but not this. A shudder shakes through my body. I don't want this. I don't want any of it. Not the ritzy neighborhood or meeting my grandmother who never could be bothered before now. I just want my small box of an apartment, my bitchy classmates, and my overprotective mom.

Charlotte unlocks the large double doors. The solid mahogany boasts what looks like handcrafted leaded glass and shiny brass door handles. Mesmerized by the elaborate knobs Charlotte uses to open both doors, I inhale sharply.

In the center of the circular foyer sits an elegant sculpted-glass table. A vase filled with white, blue, and yellow feathery flowers sits on the round top. We walk straight through and to a bright white room decorated with light-blue accents.

"This is the great room," Charlotte gushes. "Your grandmother likes to have her tea here in the afternoon."

Charlotte continues to speak, but my eyes are transfixed by a large set of windows that overlook a section of Tampa Bay. I'm drawn to them as I remember bits and pieces of memories my mom shared with me about her time here. I walk closer and stare out into the vast empty space before me. I take in the bay front, where the moon hangs high over the water's reflection. For a split second, I forget why I'm here, then a wave of emotion hits me as I view the beach-front below.

It reminds me of the only story my mother told me about my father. About how they met. About how they fell in love. Before I have a chance to dive deeper into those memories, I hear Charlotte clear her throat.

"Do you like it?" Charlotte asks, hope filling her voice.

I search for the words, trying to decide how exactly one should reply to a question that sounds so simple. But my life feels anything but simple right now.

When I don't respond, the excitement on her face slips into something more sympathetic. "I'll give you the grand tour tomorrow. I imagine you must want to get some rest."

I give a pinched smile, feeling somewhat guilty for not matching her emotion. "Actually, I'd like to take a walk on the beach."

Charlotte's brows fold in, revealing her disapproval. "But it's late."

I shrug. "I've been in a car all day, and I'm wide awake."

Charlotte nods. "Well, all right then. Let me show you the best path."

THREE

The second I reach the sand, there's a release inside me I know I've needed. I take a deep breath, sucking in the salty sea-blown air. My toes sink into the sand with each step, the tiny grains exfoliating my skin as I glide effortlessly toward the shore. It's easy to lose myself to the gentle breeze, but that's not really why I wanted to come out here.

I move blindly toward the water, peeling my black leggings and tank top from my body and tossing them aside. I free myself into the bay, like submerging myself in its depths will somehow wash away the pain and bring me closer to my mother. After all, this is where it all began.

My heart catches in my throat as I put all my energy into each stroke, all the while recalling the story my mom once told me about how she met my father. The first memory my mom, Grace, had was of when she woke up on the shore in Apollo Beach at sixteen years old. Right here, right in front of George and Rose Summer's home. Rose's son, Paul, carried her inside.

Grace didn't know where she had come from or who her parents were. All she could remember was her name, her age, and that there had been an accident, but she couldn't recall any specifics.

Rose insisted on caring for the young girl, at least until they could help her find out where she came from. Months later, the search for Grace's past was finally exhausted, and she became a permanent member of the Summer family. It was all such a strange and fateful turn of events, especially for the boy who had pulled her out of the water.

Grace had a crush on Paul from the moment she'd laid eyes on him, but Paul looked at Grace as no more than the strange orphan girl who lived in his home. Unbeknownst to him, he'd already fallen for her. And the more time he spent with her, the more he began to see it for himself. They became friends first, and then one day, when they were taking a dip in the bay, Grace got caught in an undertow. Paul was right there to save her; he pulled her out of the water and held her in his arms—then he kissed her.

From that moment on, Grace and Paul fell madly in love, and as they continued to live under the same roof, they tried to keep it from Rose and George. It was no secret.

Once they graduated from high school, Paul proposed to Grace, and they married a year later. Just six months after the wedding, on an autumn day, Grace found out she was pregnant. After Grace gave birth to a beautiful baby girl, the fighting began. Paul disappeared, and a heartbroken Grace took her baby and moved to Spring Lake to start a new life.

Beyond that, I don't have any of the details. While I've

always been curious about my father and grandparents, I could tell how upsetting the few conversations we'd had were for my mom. Quelling all that curiosity is partly what fueled my emotions during incidents like the one that happened with Steve.

I don't know how long I've been swimming when I push up from the water and open my eyes. I blink and spin in a full circle, trying to get a glimpse of the beach. Nothing. Only water surrounds me for as far as I can see. Panic sets in, sending my heart crashing into my ribs so loudly that it's all I can hear. I swipe the water away from my eyes and try to make out something, anything, that will give me a clue as to how to get back. Surely, the lights from the homes along the beach would be enough for me to find my way home. But I'm still coming up empty.

How could I have swum so far out that all shoreline sights would be lost? I don't even swim that well, according to my old gym teacher. But there's no mistaking the eerie darkness as I desperately search my surroundings.

I take a deep breath, trying to get my heart to slow enough for me to utilize my senses. When that doesn't work, I do what my mother taught me when my anger first started to get me into trouble. I close my eyes and focus on my breathing. Deep and slow, in and out.

"You can do it. You are in control, Katrina. Never forget that." I can almost sense her calming presence, hear her gentle but firm words, and feel her warm hand as it run up and down my spine.

When I open my eyes again, a stillness takes over my senses. Even the water around me seems to go completely calm as I suck in a deep, comforting breath. Then I see lights from the bay shore. Next I hear music coming from one of the neighboring homes. Finally, I feel the current pushing me in the direction I need to go. Relief rushes through me.

I swim back to shore and step out of the water on wobbly legs, then I throw on my clothes and look over at my grandmother's manor. Once again, I'm hit by its size. Even from here, it stands out from the others, especially from the homes that have been robbed of a sandy beachfront and are instead protected by a retaining walls of rocks.

Still reeling from my swim, I decide to walk it off before returning to Summer Manor. I trudge along the shore, escaping the quiet darkness of my thoughts and focusing instead on my surroundings. The music I could hear earlier seems to be coming from up ahead. I continue in that direction, and eventually, I catch sight of a group of guys are playing what seems to be a competitive game of volleyball, while a group of girls cheer them on from the pool deck above. My focus is drawn to a bronze statue of the earth goddess, Gaia, resting at one end of the pool. Her hair rises to the sky in the shape of tree roots with birds perched atop them. She's pressing a handful of feathers to her chest, her chin cast down.

Turning back to the game, my eyes lock on the ball as the guys lob it into the air, passing it back and forth more than a dozen times before one of them finally misses.

"You're a lucky bastard, Alec. Let me see you try that again," one boy taunts. "I won't miss this time."

"C'mon, Brett," one of the girls says with a laugh. "Don't be a sore loser."

Brett tosses a glare up at her then flips her off.

Meanwhile, Alec is chuckling while playfully tossing the ball into the air and catching it. "We'll see about that." Alec winks.

A fluttering erupts in my chest. The boy, Alec, is gorgeous, with a charming full-blown smile, short wavy hair, tanned skin made evident in the house lights they play under, and an athletic build that has me curious as to his age. They all appear to be around the same age as me, but I can't be sure from just one glance.

A moment later, the game is back in session. There's some laughing, some grunting, and even some cursing each time one of them misses. While Brett looks to be in a competitive match, Alec seems to be just having fun with it. But when Alec jumps into the air and brings his palm down hard on the ball, my jaw falls open as it zooms over the net, angling for the ground at Brett's feet.

Brett is already diving for it, anticipating its landing. I hold my breath and imagine the ball denting the beach while he overshoots his aim and misses it completely. *Miss it.* My mind echoes the words as my gaze follows the movement of the ball. I'm so focused on what's going to happen next, it almost feels as if time slows. *Miss it,* my mind chants. *Miss the ball.*

Brett slides too far forward, causing his clenched fists to miss the ball completely. The ball comes down hard, smacking him square on the head. A resounding pop sounds through the air, and the girls from the balcony above laugh hysterically.

They all seem so focused on the game, I have every

intention of walking away unnoticed, but I'm not fast enough. As if he senses my presence, Alec turns and finds me in the darkness. He tilts his head then—to my horror—takes a step in my direction.

All I can think to do is run. Maybe it's my soaked-through clothes, my bare feet, or the sheer and utter embarrassment that floods me from being caught snooping on the group of friends, but I can't seem to make my feet move. I'm glued to the spot, stunned as my gaze locks on the boy moving in my direction. Our eyes connect, and it's like my insides freeze too. There's an unmistakable intensity to his gaze, reminding me of the runner from earlier. But this is different, like an electric current slithering through every nerve ending of my body until I can't deny it anymore.

A jolt zaps through me like lightning—so hard and fast, I drop to my knees. Pressure mounts behind my eyes as I force them closed and press my palms against my ears. My mouth opens, as if I'll scream, but no sound follows. The pain is excruciating, and a flash of bright white light illuminates my darkened vision. It flashes over and over and over. I don't know how many times it strikes, but each one feels like a mini-electrocution.

After what seems like an eternity, the light holds—a solid white expanse accompanied by an overwhelming sense of peace. Then I'm sinking.

What I see next makes no sense, but it's as clear as the moon that hangs over the bay. Sand holds my feet prisoner as I sink into the earth while the wind swirls viciously around me. The ocean waves crash onto the shore, and all I can do is watch it in solitude. I make out voices—no, screams from somewhere else on the beach. Turning, I try to see where the commotion is coming from. All I see in the near distance are orange flames and a screen of billowing black smoke that envelops me all at once.

I'm suffocating. My hands rush to my neck. I can't breathe. I'm falling into the sand, completely helpless.

The screams grow louder as I grow immensely weaker. All I can think is that this is how it ends. Then I collapse.

In the next instant, the horrific scene vanishes, along with the white light that took me there in the first place. I gasp like it's my first breath after nearly drowning, and I'm back on the beach. I squeeze my eyes shut, suffocating the pain and suffering that couldn't have been real. But it can't be real. It was just one of my awful nightmares.

Except... I wasn't asleep. I was wide awake when the scene took over all my senses. My chest heaves as I try to rid the vision from my mind.

What just happened?

"Hey!" a voice says. "Are you okay?"

I open my eyes. A figure is rushing toward me. I then remember where I was before I escaped this reality for another. The music. The volleyball game. The boy. Alec.

I refuse to look at him, to let him see me like this. He already caught me watching his game, and now this. How embarrassing. But while I know I should be humiliated by what just happened, that isn't the feeling that swells in the deepest parts of me. I'm terrified above anything else. That vision felt entirely too real to just wave away with a shake of my head. *What is going on with me?*

"Can you hear me?" Alec drops onto the sand in front of me. "Talk to me."

The panic in the stranger's voice shakes me enough that I can finally respond. "I'm fine. I'm okay. I don't—" I raise my chin and meet his gaze, the impact of our eyelock being enough to make me completely forget what I was about to say. The attraction I felt for him earlier doesn't even compare to what I feel right now.

Concern floods his gorgeous face as his eyes scan my body. "You sure? That was quite the fall."

The embarrassment I felt earlier resurfaces, and I try to hide the heat climbing up my neck with an awkward laugh. "I'm okay, really. Thank you, though." It takes some effort to stand, so much that dizziness overtakes me, and I fall again, this time landing in his awaiting arms.

"Whoa," he says gently. "Take your time."

I look up at him, this time focusing on the guy staring down at me. His hazel-green eyes, even in the badly illuminated night, are clear. His short wavy hair frames his unspoiled face. And the natural smile that pushes up his lips wraps around my heart and squeezes.

I've stared at him too long.

"Hey." His voice is deep and calming like melted chocolate.

"I-I'm sorry. I don't know what happened. I had a long car ride here. I must be tired." I'm shocked by how together I sound after the events of tonight. I'm seeing things, experiencing electric shocks through my body, and now I'm calm? Impossible.

I'm able to sit up now, so he settles me, and we sit

together. He starts to search me for damage, but I scoot away a few inches, afraid of what he'll find if he examines me too closely. When his eyes fall back on mine, I find comfort in them immediately. *Who is this guy?*

"I was already coming over to say hello when I saw you fall," he explains. "You looked like you were in pain. I just wanted to make sure you were okay. Are you okay?" His voice is gentle, and there's something about his eyes that tells me his friendliness is genuine.

"Yeah, it was just a, um, headache, I think." I don't know why I'm choosing to be vague right now, but it seems like the right thing to do. "It hit me out of nowhere. And then I fell. And it just seemed to... linger."

The boy nods, his brows bent together like he's not sure if he should believe me. "Maybe I should take you to the hospital. Those kinds of headaches aren't normal."

With a shake of my head, I edge away from him. "Thank you, but I'll be fine. I already feel better." I stand effortlessly to prove it.

He looks unsure but rises with me. "Can I at least walk you back to where you came from?" He nods to my grandmother's manor, causing unease to snake through me.

"Um..." I start awkwardly. "How did you know where my home is? I just moved here today."

"You're Rose's granddaughter, right?" He says it confidently, but there's also something else there I'm struggling to detect. Disapproval?

I shake away the thoughts. Now is not the time to make assumptions about the thoughts of a boy I don't even know. "That would be me."

"We've been expecting you."

My insides jump at that comment. "You have?" Then I shake my head, realizing I have a more important question. "Did you say 'we'?"

Alec nods then throws a look over his shoulder. I follow his gaze to find Alec's friends all huddled together, staring at us. The guys look genuinely curious, but I can't shake the hasty glares the girls cast in my direction.

"You've kind of been the talk of the town," Alec says with a sheepish smile. "It's the curse of moving to a small town, I guess."

I let out an awkward laugh.

"C'mon, already," one of the girls calls out to Alec. "We're going inside to watch a movie."

"Yeah, man," one of the guys says with a grin. "Bring your new friend if you want. She's cute."

Heat rushes to my cheeks at the compliment, and Alec lifts his brows as if that's not a bad idea. "Well, what do you say, new girl? Want to make some friends?"

A whispered argument strikes up between the members of the group behind him. I'm sure they think I can't hear them. I make out every single word, and it's enough to solidify the fact that I'm as unwelcome in this town as I was back in Silver Lake. I try not to feel dejected about that small fact, but it's close to impossible.

I take a step backward and shake my head. "I really should get going. It's late, and Charlotte is waiting for me." I start to turn away, but first, I sneak a look at him from under my eyelashes. "It was nice meeting you."

"Nice meeting you…"

I walk away quickly, ignoring his voice when he calls from behind me. "Wait. Let me at least walk you home."

I refuse to let Alec waste another second on me when I know my time here is limited. My birthday is in one month. I'll be eighteen and free to leave this place. And that's exactly what I plan to do.

FOUR

aybe I was rude to take off like that when Alec was nothing but nice to me, but this situation is much too strange to explain to a complete stranger, especially one whose name I didn't even ask for but overheard, nonetheless. Then again, he didn't ask for mine either. But none of that matters. Something tells me I will see him again soon.

Charlotte is standing at the great room window when I enter the house. I half expect a lecture for staying out too late, but she smiles easily and leads me up the white marble staircase. At the far end of the hall, she opens a set of double doors with a grand flourish.

The bedroom is an overabundance of riches, with floor-to-ceiling windows filling a rounded wall that faces the bay, a gold four-poster bed with fluffy white bedding, dozens of gold-framed photos on the wallpapered walls, sculptures, and various pieces of distressed furniture. I meet my own gaze in the vanity's oval mirror. The ornate looking glass might just be the most beautiful piece in the room. With its intricately carved gold frame and hand-sculpted design, it stands out from everything else in the room by far.

My mousy brown hair is all knotted and windblown. I consider taking the gold-plated brush to it, wishing it were longer so I could pull it up into a bun and let my neck breathe. But while I'm in my grandmother's home and this is my room for the time being, I feel like I'm an intruder.

I look back up at my reflection and consider my complexion. I think this is the first time I've really looked at myself in months. My skin is pastier than normal, and my dull gray eyes still hint at life despite being bloodshot from lack of sleep. My cheekbones are still too pointy, and the corners of my mouth are naturally turned down to the point where I'm always being asked to smile even when nothing is wrong.

"You're young and beautiful, Katrina," my mom once said. "Those thoughts inside your head that tell you you're not are simply a lie. But you'll never see the truth until you stop looking at your reflection." She pinned my cheeks between her fingers and tapped my chest. "This is where your true mirror lies. Look here."

Turning away from the mirror—and the painful memory—I watch as Charlotte crosses the room and steps in front of another set of double doors.

She pushes them open before turning to me with a smile. "Your bathroom. I'm sure you'd like to wash up before bed."

I say nothing as my gaze slips past the petite blond woman and catches sight of an oversized walk-in closet and a pearl garden tub beside a giant glass walk-in shower.

"Well then," Charlotte says when I still haven't responded. "I'll leave you be." She steps past me, slips out my bedroom doors, and looks back at me with a hand on each door in preparation of closing them. "Breakfast is served at eight. Your grandmother is never late." With a final look of playful warning, she closes the doors, leaving me to myself.

Not wanting to wait any longer to escape this overwhelming reality, I tear off my clothes and climb under the covers. It doesn't take long for my lids to grow heavy with exhaustion.

THE MAHOGANY VANITY in my dreams is a magnified version of the one I remember. Much like everything else in my new room, this one towers over me. If the objects aren't generous in size, then they make up for it with their beauty and fragility. I've never felt farther from home.

Staring back at me from the large oval mirror is a reflection of a girl who looks like me. Her face is warmer than mine, like a nice olive-tone that reminds me of my mother. There's almost a glow about it that I can't turn away from. Her eyes are a bright, electric shade of silver. Her dark-brown hair is shiny and thick, flowing down past her shoulders. I take in her groomed features with awe. Physically, despite my mom's warning, which enters deep in my subconscious, she's everything I wish to be.

I reach out for the glass, and with every inch distance my arm creeps toward it, my reflection follows in perfect synchrony. I halt my movement, and she halts too. She copies me as I raise my hand to my face then move a strand of hair away from my eye. I gasp, and she gasps too. That's when I realize... the girl in the mirror is me.

I'm almost afraid to lean in, but I want to get a closer look. My lashes are longer. My nails, now near my face, appear manicured and long. But that's not all that's different. There's a necklace. The green stone reflects a shard of light from the glass chandelier, and I realize it's not just any stone. It's dainty, rare, and exquisite. It most definitely doesn't belong to me, yet it sits perfectly above the swell of my breasts as if it were made for me.

I reach for the jewel to lift it from my chest and examine it, but the moment I touch it, the stone glows from within. I release it, my heart pounding like a steady drum. Glancing back up at my reflection, I widen my eyes in surprise. The image, no longer my own, smiles back at me with an almost evil glimmer in her eye. Fear erupts inside me, and I can feel myself shaking. Meanwhile, my image does not shake with me. Instead, she smiles brighter.

The girl's eyes narrow on me then turn so they no longer meet mine. She's now staring over my shoulder at a maroon-and-white antique vase laden with fresh flowers. The girl points her finger directly at it. It's not until she begins to raise her arm that I realize what is happening. As her finger rises, so does the vase in the reflection, higher and higher until the vase is lingering in midair.

As her eyes snap back to me, the streaks of madness in them freeze me completely. She isn't smiling anymore. The green necklace around her neck is glowing so brightly that sparks of light are spraying from its center. Then she opens her mouth into a grotesque shape just before letting out a terrifying scream.

I jam my palms against my ears in an attempt to muffle the horrible noise. It's impossible. I know I'll never shake the sound, and it seems to be only getting louder. As the girl's pitch reaches a crescendo, the vase in the reflection shakes violently until it shatters in midair, spraying my bedroom with glass.

STILL COVERING MY EARS, and with my eyelids pinched closed, I scream myself awake. I continue to scream until someone starts shaking me.

My eyes shoot open, my body stiffening in defense as if the girl in the mirror will attack me, but she's no longer there. I'm in bed, covered from head to toe in sweat. It was all just a dream.

It's Charlotte who woke me. She holds me, shushing me as I sob. "It was just a dream. It's okay. Everything is going to be fine."

"Fine?" I squeal. My eyes fly open, and I shake my head. The voice beside me is calm and understanding, and I feel anything but. "You think everything is going to be fine? My mom is dead. I'm living in this"—my eyes fly around the room—"ridiculously expensive mansion with a woman I've never met. And I'm having all these crazy dreams and visions, and—" I stop myself when my thoughts conjure up an image of the jogger in the black cap. I don't know what that was, but that didn't feel normal either. How he glared at me, like he already hated me after just one glance.

"Visions, you say?"

I turn to look at the short-haired blond woman and shake my head, deciding it's best not to elaborate. "I don't know what I just woke up from, but that was not a dream."

Charlotte places her hand on my back. I turn to look at her just as she averts her eyes, causing a knot to form in my gut. Something in her face goes beyond the kind, gentle woman I first met. She's hiding something. I can see it on her guarded expression.

"You've been through a lot, Katrina. I expect you'll have many more unpleasant dreams."

"I sure as hell hope not."

Charlotte snaps her head to look at me and softens her eyes. "I understand that you're angry, but your grandmother won't approve of that language. Not in this house."

I bite my tongue before I spit back a retort that Charlotte doesn't deserve. She's right. I'm angry. I'm saying things I shouldn't. But how can anyone expect that any of this is normal?

With another shake of my head, I sigh. "I'm going to try to get some sleep now. Maybe we can start over in the morning."

The smile that spreads across her face warms my insides despite current events. "I'd like that very much, Kat." She pats my knee above the comforter, then she stands and hands me a teacup filled with steaming liquid. *When did that get here?*

"It's my special concoction. I promise this will help you get a good night's sleep. I meant to give it to you earlier."

I don't spend any more time questioning how or when the tea arrived at my bedside. I take a few slow sips and thank Charlotte as she's closing the door to my room. Then I lay my head back on my pillow and easily fall asleep.

FIVE

The moment I begin my descent of the grand staircase, my mouth tingles at the aroma of bacon and eggs. I'm still groggy from the long trip and lack of sleep, but thankfully, no other dreams haunted me during the night. I follow the scent past the white great room, through a brilliant mahogany arch, and into a lavish dining room decorated in a sea of electric blue—from the plates on the wall to the table coverings and oversized candles on them. I'm mesmerized by it all.

Charlotte greets me at the dining room entrance with a smile. "Good morning, Kat. You look well rested. Your grandmother had to run a quick errand this morning, so I thought I'd give you a tour while we wait."

"Okay, sure."

I don't tell Charlotte how angry my stomach is with hunger. Instead, I let her lead me all over the much-too-large house, trying to not let my jaw drop over every exquisite detail. The main floor is daunting in itself, with what Charlotte told me was a thirty-foot-high coffered ceiling, supported by cast Italian stone columns. They extend all the way to the upper-floor gallery, where the great room over-looks a breathtaking view of the bay and the endless sea beyond it.

Charlotte takes me past the foyer and grand staircase into another section of the house, skipping a narrow hallway. "What's down there?"

"Oh, that's Rose—er, your grandmother's quarters. Rose prefers to not take the stairs, so if you ever need her, this is where you'll find her—in her bedroom, her study, or the library. They're all down there."

"Library?" My curiosity is immediately piqued.

Charlotte lights up, her eyes practically glowing with excitement. "Oh, yes. And it's by far the most charming room in the entire house. I'll leave that up to your grandmother to show you herself, but I'll let her know you're eager to see it. Come with me."

She continues the tour, showing me the many guest bedrooms, her arts-and-crafts room, and a giant darkroom with theater seating and a projection screen on one wall.

Then she turns to me and claps her hands. "That's pretty much it for the tour. You've seen the pool and the beach. This is your home now, Kat. We'd very much like for you to feel comfortable here, so if there's anything you need, please let me know."

Staring back at the woman, I wonder for the hundredth time in the past week who exactly she is to my grandmother. What is a "caretaker," and what are her responsibilities to Summer Estate—and now to me?

We're on our way back downstairs when I can't help but ask, "Why such a large home? This place is gorgeous and all, but I can't imagine one person needing"—I sweep my arms around me—"all of this."

"Rose and your grandfather lived in Apollo Beach most of their lives. Their parents were the best of friends and all traveled from Greece to build the School of Gaia, a private college here. After she married your grandfather, they took what their parents built and expanded the community, which Rose now oversees. She has her hands in many areas —politics, real estate, education, and the environment. I suppose that all comes with a certain status that's critical for her to uphold." Charlotte is clearly being cautious as she answers.

"You make it sound like Rose owns this town."

Charlotte shrugs. "Some say she does. Overall, your grandmother is a very well respected woman here."

"Overall?"

Charlotte smiles. "Well, let's just say there are a number of folks in this town who don't love the idea of a woman running things. After George passed, it seems she's never stopped having to prove herself."

"Really? Why?"

Charlotte shrugs. "I'll never understand it, but ever since the fire, Rose has had to deal with insurmountable pressure from the community. And it's never let up."

"Wait. What fire?"

Charlotte's eyes flit away from mine, her eyebrows slightly furrowed. "Your mom never told you about the fire? Rose and your grandfather had a section of the house remodeled because of it."

I shake my head, and discomfort churns in my stomach.

Why is it starting to feel like my mom kept so many secrets from me? "Not a word. Like I told you, she didn't tell me much."

Charlotte sighs. "Right. I guess she wouldn't have had a reason to share that. I shouldn't have assumed you knew. Forget I said anything. Rose will surely tell you all about it in good time."

My jaw drops. "You can't do that, Charlotte. I want to know about the fire. What happened? When?"

Charlotte frowns, the deep creases between her eyes showing her worry. "I really should let Rose tell you, Kat. It's her story, not mine. I'm sorry I mentio—"

"Oh my gosh, Charlotte. Just tell me what you know," I beg. "Unless you want me to start digging around on the internet and believe everything I read."

Charlotte's eyes flash with worry before she lets out a heavy sigh and casts a long, stern look at me. "All right, all right." Her voice is hushed and her eyes narrowed as if Rose might overhear her from wherever she is. "A little over ten years ago, there was an awful fire in the estate. No one knows how it started, but your grandfather was in the library when it all began. He was trapped for so long that everyone began to believe he was dead. Rose finally got to him and pulled him out. He was alive, but his condition worsened over time, and respiratory issues killed him a year later. Rose didn't want to leave the place she and your grandfather had built, so she sought help to care for Summer Manor. That's how I came into the picture."

My heart aches from such a tragic story of my poor grandfather. I wish I could have met him. Maybe my mom didn't know about the fire. Surely, she would have wanted to visit after hearing something like that. Even as my questions and thoughts compile, I realize I'm trying to make sense out of something I haven't even begun to understand. From how my mom had made it sound, George Summer loved her like a father, and in return, she cared for him deeply.

Charlotte must have said all that she's willing to say, because she leads me past the great room, and through an archway that leads to a formal dining room. Through the next set of wide-open doors, I spot a gourmet kitchen with beautifully ornate cabinets and sparkling countertops. It's clear there isn't a spot in this house that isn't meticulously looked after.

That feeling of just how out of place I am here snakes through me all over again, but I have no time to dwell on it. Moments after we've stepped into the dining room, the sound of the front door opening and shutting has my attention. My heart starts to race. All the anticipation and buildup about meeting Rose has done a number on my nerves.

Charlotte pops onto her toes as excitement lights up her face. "Oh, good. She's back. Time for breakfast." She scrambles over to the nearest seat and pulls it out for me. "Go on. Have a seat. I'll run and get the food."

I take my seat as she runs out of the room just as a stranger—my grandmother—enters the room, makes her way around the table, and sits across from me. The corners of her mouth are slightly upturned, but I'm struggling to figure out if she's smiling or not.

She doesn't say a word while she looks me over as if trying to remember me from some past life. I do the same to her. With cotton-ball hair, dark-gray eyes, and the skin of a middle-aged woman, she is, in fact, a stunning sight. The woman may be in her upper sixties, but she doesn't look a day over fifty.

While I feel like I'm staring back at a stranger, Rose's curious expression makes me feel as if she doesn't consider me a stranger at all.

"You are more beautiful than I imagined." She speaks articulately, matter-of-factly, and with a tinge of a Greek accent. "It's as if I'm looking at your mother's reflection."

As nervous as I am, I find the strength to respond. "Is it? I was always curious about what my mother looked like when she was younger. She didn't have any photos."

Rose brightens as she nods. "Well, you are the spitting image." She leans back slightly and reaches for her glass of water. "I have plenty of photos. You're welcome to all of them."

Relief makes its way through me. I don't know what I expected to feel when I met Rose, but she isn't nearly as intimidating as I imagined. "Thank you—" I nearly call her Grandma, but I stop myself. "Is it okay if I call you Rose?"

Rose wrinkles her nose and waves a hand in the air. "Of course. Whatever makes you comfortable, dear." Her gaze drops to where I'm tugging on my bracelet, still trying to remove it from my wrist like a dirty stain. "Is that what I think it is?"

"It was my mother's." I look down at it, focusing on the clasp. "The clasp is broken though, and the chain is strong. I can't seem to remove it."

"Perhaps you should take it as a sign."

I meet Rose's gaze. "She gave this to me the day she died." My chest feels shaky with emotion. "I don't want to wear it anymore."

"But you must, Katrina. Your mother never took it off, and neither should you."

I frown. "But she doesn't even know where it came from."

Rose nods. "She always believed it kept her safe. It will keep you safe too."

My breath catches in my chest at how much Rose knows. "That's just a silly superstition. Look what happened as soon as she removed it. She died. I don't want that reminder."

My grandmother's eyes soften. "You shouldn't think of it as a burden. It was a gift, the last thing your mother ever gave you, and she did so with good intention. The meaning behind that should never be lost. If it was your mother's final wish for you to wear it, then that's what you will do." Then her cheeks lift enough for me to know she's attempting to lighten the mood. "You must be starved. I believe Charlotte whipped us up some of your favorites."

I think I catch a wink from Rose, but it happens so quickly, I can't be sure. My stomach tightens. *How does she know what my favorites are?* Rose looks over her shoulder just as Charlotte walks out with a large tray of food. I see bacon, eggs, and waffles with a side of blueberries. Not exactly the most original meal, but the meal is, in fact, my favorite.

Charlotte doesn't join us to eat as I expect. Instead, she leaves us to our meal and walks back into the kitchen.

I fumble my napkin as I unfold it and place it on my lap. If there's one thing my mom taught me well, it's proper manners. If only I can get my nerves to cooperate, I might stand a chance of disguising my natural awkwardness. I pick up my fork and lift my gaze back to Rose. "You have a beautiful home." I can't help but wonder if she knows how my mom and I lived back in Silver Lake.

"Thank you, Katrina. I do hope you will make yourself comfortable. This is your home now too."

I nod, appreciative of her hospitality, while also calculating when the right time will be to tell Rose that I don't plan to stay for long.

"Oh, and don't worry, dear," Rose says as she raises her fork to take a bite of egg. "Charlotte will show you around town, and you'll make fast friends. Just in time for school to start up in the fall." Rose peers up at me over her fork. "I'm not sure what you were planning to do about school when you were in Silver Lake, but there's a lovely private school on the island that will be happy to take you."

I freeze. Humiliation accompanied by shock washes over me as I think about how to tell Rose that college isn't in my future. Not now. Not ever. Not even if I wanted to go. "Well, um, there's something I should probably tell you."

Rose sets her fork down and rests her hands in her lap. "Katrina, you should know that moving here gives you a clean slate. At everything. Your friendships, your education, your future. And I'll help you however I can, every step of the way."

Her words and tone are so genuinely kind, but I get the feeling she knows things no one could have possibly told her. It doesn't matter, though. I shake my head, refusing to believe that I deserve what she's offering. I won't take her pity. I'm not a charity case she can buy affection from because she suddenly cares about my wellbeing. Where has she been all these years? I can feel my insides start to quake.

"You don't know what you're saying. There are things about me you'd never understand, that no amount of therapy could ever fix. I got kicked out of school for throwing a boy out a window. And then my mom died before I could finish high school. Even if I wanted to go to college, I couldn't." I avert my eyes from hers, look down at my plate, and start shoving food into my mouth as fast as I can. The sooner I feed my angry stomach, the sooner I can escape this room before my emotions get the better of me.

The silence that follows stretches for so long that I nearly choke on my bite of blueberries when I hear her speak again.

"I understand more than you know." Her tone is quiet, but the intensity behind her words shakes my bones. "Soon, you'll come to understand it too."

I look up at my grandmother, her cryptic message making me see her in a whole new light. It's like she already has an agenda for me, one she doesn't plan on giving me any say in.

Charlotte steps quietly back into the room, her eyes darting between us. "Can I get you two anything else?"

Rose's gaze roams over me. "Perhaps you and Katrina could head to the island today. I'm sure you could use some new... items."

I look at Charlotte then back at Rose. I brought my entire wardrobe from back home, so it's unnecessary to go shopping so soon. "Thank you, Rose, but I have clothes. You don't need to buy me anything."

"Nonsense, dear. You are not on vacation. Surely, you'll need things for the summer. I insist. I would take you myself, but my week is jam-packed with events. Charlotte will take you and show you around the island. It's where everyone in town hangs out."

I think that's the third time she's mentioned an "island," and I'm just now questioning it. "Are you talking about an actual island? We're on the bay coast. There aren't any islands around here."

Rose's eyes light up like a million bulbs switched on at once. "Well, then I insist you go today and see it for yourself. What do you think, Charlotte?"

"I think it's a wonderful idea," Charlotte says.

I take a peek over my grandmother's shoulder at Charlotte, who is giving me one of her comforting smiles.

"It will be fun, I promise. I'll show you around. We'll look in a few stores, grab some lunch, maybe get our nails done. Just a girls' day out."

It feels rude to reject their offer any more than I already have. With a quiet sigh and a forced smile, I agree to the plan.

"Well, that's settled," Rose says before rising from the table. "I'm afraid I must jet off again. Let's have tea tomorrow, shall we? There's something I'd like to show you."

I'm starting to see why the town is so intimidated by Rose. She's as fierce as she is kind, as assertive as she is observant, and as understanding as she is convincing. It's strange, but even after going my entire life without knowing my grandmother, something about her feels familiar to me. And it's as if she's known me my whole life.

SIX

"I'm ready whenever you are," I say to Charlotte when I touch down at the bottom of the staircase.

After the nerve-racking morning with Rose, I'm not as opposed to getting out of the house as I was initially. In fact, I could use the distraction from my thoughts. It seems distractions are all I have these days, and it's all starting to feel a little dark. My mom would want better for me. I want better for myself, even if that means stepping outside of my comfort zone.

We walk out the main door and down the front steps then hop into the white Escalade. I don't know what it is about the sight of the tiny woman climbing into a giant SUV, but a light laugh pushes up my throat.

Charlotte looks at me with amused curiosity. "What's so funny?"

I shake my head then wave around the vehicle. "It's just so... obnoxiously big, isn't it? Like Rose's home, and—" I start to wonder if I'm being rude and let out a sigh. "I'm just not used to all of this. I don't feel comfortable letting Rose spend her money on me. It must already be such an inconvenience having me stay here. But I'll be eighteen soon and then—"

"Stop." Charlotte turns her full body to face me and holds my gaze for an intense few seconds, enough to tell me that whatever she's about to say is serious. "You are blood, Katrina. You are a Summer. You have no idea what that means today, but you will. Whatever happened with your family in the past has nothing to do with you. You're here because Rose wants you to be here. She's always wanted to be a part of your life. I agree, the circumstances are unfortunate, but in no way are you a burden. Quite the opposite, in fact."

I shake my head, refusing to believe it.

"It's true," Charlotte says firmly. "I've never seen Rose like this. So lively, so... happy. It's like she's found her passion again."

I frown. "What? How?"

"Ever since George died, her responsibilities to this town have become her life. She stopped remembering why she started all this work to begin with. She doesn't even leave Apollo Beach anymore. I have a feeling your presence is already changing that. So enjoy today, will you? If anything, do it for me." She winks, resetting the mood. "I could use a fun day out."

Tension releases from my body, and I lean back into my seat. "Fine. But I'm looking for a job while we're out."

"Now, there's a great idea."

With a satisfied smile, Charlotte drives us out of the Summer Estates gate and goes straight to where we had taken a left at the T last night. From what I can tell, this is the entire town, a T-shape with carved-out inlets that make up waterfront housing developments. We drive past the public beach, where a long rock structure juts into the ocean. Huge waves crash over the end of it, sending water spraying high into the air.

Past that is a row of large coastal homes that appear dated compared to the ones in Summer Estates. In fact, the farther down the road we travel, the older the houses seem to get. One house in particular sticks out like a sore thumb. It looks completely abandoned, with chipped paint, angled shutters, boarded-up windows, tall weeds for grass, and overgrown pathways. Yet, I can see past the distress and visualize the beautiful landmark it once probably was. But even as it is, I'm strangely comforted by the sight. To know this town isn't the immaculate storybook land I initially thought is enough to ground me back into reality.

My eyes are still focused out the window on Charlotte's side as we pass another public beach, this one clearly not as well cared for as the one near Summer Estates. It's completely deserted, save for a man dressed in all black. It's him.

My pulse takes off racing. From the T-shirt that stretches around his muscles, to the cap he wears low enough to cover his eyes, and to black slacks that make me desperately want to know where he's headed, there's no question that it's the jogger from last night—the older guy with the unforgettably harsh glare.

I'm relieved he doesn't look at me this time as we pass. Letting him catch me staring the first time was almost too embarrassing to handle. I don't think I would survive it again.

"Here we are."

Charlotte's voice cuts through my racing thoughts, and I look forward to find the landscape changing before my very eyes. As we escape the last of the worn-down section of the neighborhood, we start to pass over an arched one-lane stone bridge. Its rails and end posts are sculpted like Greek pillars with a statue of Apollo and his bow perched on each one.

Beyond the end of the bridge sits a castle-sized black iron gate with "Summer Island" written in metallic gold above it. A matching gold Greek sun with an *S* separates at the middle when the doors begin to open.

"Summer Island? You've got to be kidding me," I mutter. "My grandparents developed this too?"

Charlotte's light infectious laughter floats through the air. "Your grandparents' parents, yes. Rose and George just added all the embellishments."

I don't even notice the guard house to the side of the gate until Charlotte slows the car and rolls down her window. "Hey, Herk. Meet Rose's granddaughter, Katrina. I'm sure you'll be seeing a lot of her."

They exchange a wink, then he leans over to smile at me. "Well, well, well. She does exist," he exclaims. "It's so lovely to finally meet you, Katrina."

"It's just Kat." I can't help but smile back at the charming and animated man.

"Of course, of course. Well, I'm Herkle. But the people around here call me whatever they want. Herk. Herkie.

Hercules." He holds up an arm, pushes up his massive bicep, then winks as if it's some inside joke.

I let out an awkward laugh, not knowing how else to respond. "It's nice to meet you, Herkle."

"Will I be seeing you at the next Encha—"

Charlotte gives him a wave, cutting him off, while starting to drive forward again. "Not yet, Herk. In time." Then she faces forward, leaving me confused, and drives through the open doors of the gate.

"What was he talking about, Charlotte?"

Charlotte shrugs and tosses me a smile. "There's a weekly event Rose runs. Kind of like a town hall meeting but a bit more exclusive. You'll attend one soon enough."

I don't want to speak my thoughts aloud. The last thing I want to do is attend a town hall event. *What would be the purpose of that?*

Large overgrown trees shade the winding pathway for what feels like miles before the branches thin out and I'm able to see the sky again. My jaw drops at what opens up before me. Among Greek-inspired buildings with a contemporary spin, temple structures make up office buildings. There are outdoor restaurants, a shopping center, and a large stadium, which holds what appears to be an athletic center of some sort, with tennis courts, basketball hoops, a track, and a pool. It's like we've entered some sort of ancient Greek paradise.

"Pretty cool, huh?" Charlotte is staring back at me with a smile that lights up her entire face. Obviously, she's proud of what my grandparents created.

I'm still wrapping my brain around the fact that my

family owns everything in this town. No wonder that Alec kid knew who I was before I ever introduced myself. *What else does everyone know?*

"Where would you like to go first? Perhaps we'll start by getting you a nice dress for your birthday."

The mention of my birthday throws off my mood some. "Why would I need a dress for that? I don't have plans."

Charlotte's eyes widen. "Oh my. Rose didn't tell you?"

I scrunch my face, confused yet again. "Tell me what? I've barely spoken with her."

"Your eighteenth birthday is a big deal, not just because of your age, but because this year, it falls on the summer solstice. We always have an elaborate party to celebrate the summer solstice." Her eyes are so big and bright, I feel like I'm supposed to make some sort of connection.

"Um, okay." I say the words slowly, trying to make sense of something. But I'm only growing more frustrated with all the secrets and insinuations that there's something big I'm missing. "I don't plan on celebrating my birthday. Whatever plans Rose has, she can cancel."

Charlotte makes a noise in the back of her throat, clearly frustrated with me. "Kat, please," she says almost desperately. "You have no idea how big of a deal this is. To your grandmother. To the town. To you—" Her face relaxes some. "Please, just humor me today. Let me get you a dress. Or, if you'd like, pick out some fabric, and I can make you one myself."

Charlotte's craft room is beginning to make sense. I let out a heavy breath, knowing my stubborn nature isn't doing anyone any good.

But when is any of this going to start making sense? Why does it always feel like I'm missing something important? I let out a sigh. "Okay. I guess a new dress won't kill me."

Charlotte's lids widen at my surrender. "Really?" She claps her hands together. "I know just the perfect place to start."

One gorgeous green dress, a pair of silver heels, and a pair of tiny diamond earrings later, Charlotte is still trying to convince me to get something in every store we go into—swimming suits, workout clothes, and casual outfits for whatever. I refuse all of it.

We're setting our purchases in the car when Charlotte tilts her head at me. "I don't suppose I can talk you into getting a mani-pedi with me, can I?"

Biting down on my smile, I shake my head then point at the three-building structure behind her with the columns that line the center building and curved stairs wrapping both sides. "Actually, I kind of wanted to check out the library."

Charlotte looks over at it then shrugs. "Okay." She fishes something out of her purse then hands me a plastic library card. "You'll need this. Meet me at Island Grille when you're done." She turns and points across the grassy courtyard that takes up the center of the island. "It's right down that gravel drive next to the marina. You can't miss it."

"Okay. In an hour?"

She nods. "See you then. Bring your appetite," she calls as she walks off, her hair flying around her face in the breeze.

I cross the street toward the library, in awe once again of

the detail put into these replica structures. My mom never mentioned how obsessed Rose was with her Greek ancestry, but it's all starting to come to light now. Between all the Summer-owned properties, Rose's home, and the touches of her heritage sprinkled throughout, my curiosity was piqued enough to want to know more.

I'm halfway across the street when I hear an engine getting louder as it gains speed down the main drive. I look over to find a red Audi convertible heading straight for me. The driver's eyes are pinned on me like I'm a target on a crash test she can't wait to nail, and her friend is laughing maniacally in the passenger seat.

What the—?

My heart speeds as I think quickly. I don't know whether to run backward or forward in an attempt to save myself from harm. All I know is that the woman behind the wheel has no intention of slowing. If anything, she's speeding up. Her chin tilts down, her eyes narrow, and her fingers lift before regripping the wheel.

I'm running out of time, and I can't help but think about my mom and wonder if this is how she felt in those final moments before she was struck.

Maybe this is how I die too.

SEVEN

I snap out of my haunting thoughts just long enough to make a decision to sprint forward, but after one step, I realize there's no time to run from the quickly approaching vehicle. Instead, I use all the energy I can muster to leap out of the street.

I didn't anticipate my strength. I fly through the air, clearing the street and sidewalk completely, then lose all control as I try to get my feet beneath me for the landing. My toes touch down on the grass, but I'm leaning too far forward. Momentum pushes me hard onto my knees, and I roll until the towering statue of Athena stops me.

"Oomph." All the air leaves my body, just as I hear the squeal of tires from applied brakes.

I look up to find two familiar-looking girls in the car, one with light brown hair, the other blond. "Sorry about that!" the blond girl in the driver's seat calls out. "I hope I didn't hurt you." The laughter in her voice tells me I shouldn't believe her. Then she speeds away with her friend hollering with laughter beside her.

I roll my eyes and stand up, dusting grass and dirt from

my black shorts and tank top. Now I remember where I know those girls from. They were at the volleyball game, cheering on Alec and Brett. I had a feeling they were trouble even then. The near hit and run incident just solidified it.

After checking my body to make sure they didn't do any real damage, I confirm all my bones are intact. In fact, there's not even a scratch on me. I blow out an annoyed breath and climb the steps to the library then stop immediately once inside.

White marble floors span the length of the three-story building. Endless rows of books surround the perimeter of each floor. The center is a wide-open space with a large glass dome ceiling that pours sunlight down onto a gold statue of the most beautiful woman I've ever seen in my life. Her hair is long and flowing. Her eyes catch the light so that they appear to glow, and her nude form reveals gracious curves. Her expression is one of someone putting up a great fight. The arm she extends is flexed, showcasing her strength, and she's holding something. It takes me a second to figure out what's in her hand, and when I do, I gasp.

A black snake with gold scales is wrapped around her fist. It looks to be hissing at her, with its mouth open wide and its reach only inches from her face. I nearly believe she's in some kind of danger. But then I realize it's the serpent that is helpless within her grip. Curious, I get closer to the statue to see if there's any information written about her. But after circling the figure a few times, looking for a plaque or anything to clue me in as to who she is, I come up empty.

"Can I help you with something, miss?"

I look at the man who just approached. "Actually, yes. Who is she? I can't find any information about her."

The man cranes his neck to look up at the statue, and by the blush that creeps onto his cheeks, it's clear I'm not the only one who finds the woman stunning. "I believe she's an ancient Greek goddess."

I frown. "Right, but do you know her name?"

He looks back at me, seeming completely thrown by my question. "No. No one knows who she is." He perks up. "But if it's Greek mythology you're interested in, I can point you in the right direction."

My curiosity fades into intrigue when I realize I can probably find the woman with a little research. "That would be great. Thank you."

The man smiles and leads me to the top floor then to a section in the back corner named Mythologies. He leaves me, and I immediately begin scouring the shelves. One of the first books I come across is about the summer solstice. I slip it out from the stacks, remembering how interested Charlotte seemed to be in the occasion. I can brush up on my knowledge at least.

The next book I find is all about gods and goddesses from ancient Greece. I pull it down, sit on the floor, and begin to thumb through it, determined to find out who the statue in the library depicts. I flip through every single page, skimming the words and focusing on the images. Disappointment fills me when I get to the end, no closer to figuring out who the mystery woman is. How strange. Sighing, I pick myself off the floor, squeeze the book back into the stacks, and continue perusing.

I've just pulled out two more books that might help feed my curiosity when I look up at the large wall clock and gasp. *Shoot.* My time is up. I take off down the aisle and round the corner, plowing headfirst into a moving target.

I stumble back. "I'm so sorry."

"Don't be. I wasn't looking."

I'm so flustered that I don't realize I've bumped into Alec until I hear his deep, familiar voice. I look up at him, causing a stampede of horses to start galloping in my chest. Even in the darkness last night, I knew he was gorgeous, but today is a different story. With the sun at his back, his green eyes practically sparkling with his smile, and his clean-cut good looks, I know I'm in trouble. "It's you."

My entire body heats so fast, I have no chance of hiding my deep humiliation. I can't believe I just said that. After the way we met last night, and now this, he must think I'm a total weirdo.

"Are we going to meet like this every time?" he jokes.

I cringe then let out an awkward laugh. "I really hope not. I am sorry, though. I was rushing to be somewhere, and I wasn't paying attention."

The corner of his mouth tips up playfully. "It's okay if you're doing these things on purpose just to talk to me." His eyes glimmer. "I don't mind."

I bite down on my smile and roll my eyes. "You're onto me." Another thought crosses my mind. "Except I've been up here for some time, while it looks like you just got here. So, maybe it's you who is trying to run into me."

This time, it's Alec's face that flushes with color. "Okay, so

I might have seen you from downstairs and come up to say hello. I didn't know you were going to throw yourself at me."

I laugh while my eyes catch on something he's holding. My books somehow found their way into his hands when we bumped into each other. "Oh, I'll take those." I reach for them, but Alec pulls them out of reach from me and glances at the one facing him.

"The summer solstice, huh? I guess you are your grandmother's daughter."

For a second, I wonder if he's trying to offend me, but that doesn't seem like something he would do. Still, his comment rubs me the wrong way. "What do you mean?"

His eyes widen like he realizes how he might have come across. "Just that your grandmother is into all that stuff. It makes sense that you would be too." When I give him a strange look, he shakes his head. "It's not weird or anything. It seems half the town is into this stuff. You would think we lived on an ancient Greek burial ground or something."

I smile and slip my books from his hands, knowing exactly what he means. "Moving here made me curious, I guess."

He pushes his hands into his pockets and rocks forward like he's nervous. As he does, a strand of curly hair falls in front of his eyes. Besides being ridiculously cute, he's also sweet and friendly, and for some reason, he came up here to talk to me. Warmth spreads in my chest.

"Curious about the solstice or Greek mythology in general?"

"Both." I shrug. "My birthday falls on the summer solstice this year, and Rose wants to have this big celebration. I don't really understand what the fascination is, but I want to try."

He gives me a smile that melts me down to my toes. "Well, it's totally cool if you're into it all. Some people around here don't get it, but I think it's cool how history and mythology blend together. My parents are fascinated with all that stuff too."

"They are?"

Alec nods. "Oh, yeah. They're herbalists, so they're all big into sacred healing rituals and holistic healing and all of that. My mom owns an herbal shop on the island, and my dad teaches ancestral herbalism at the private college. I don't know if they're quite as intense about it as Rose, but it all stems from the same beliefs, I think."

I nod, sensing he has something more to say. But judging by the bend of his brows, he's figuring out how to word it.

After too much time passes, unease shakes through me, and I give a shaky laugh. "Is there something you want to ask me?"

His eyelids spread wide, and his mouth opens. "Um, no." He shakes his head. "It's not important."

I push my lips to the side and frown. "Just ask. Is it about my grandmother? Or me?"

Alec shuffles his feet. "Now that you're putting me on the spot, I wish I never even thought about it. I don't want to offend you."

I straighten my shoulders and look him dead in the eyes. "You don't even know me. There's no possible way you can offend me."

He releases a breath. "Okay. It's just... people around

here call your grandmother a Wiccan or whatever"—he nods at the books in my hands—"because she's so obsessed with all of that. They think she's into witchcraft and stuff." He lets out an awkward laugh. "Crazy, right?"

I open my mouth to tell him she's not into anything like that, but then I snap it shut, realizing I actually have no idea what Rose's religious beliefs are. "To be honest, I don't know Rose well enough to speak on her behalf, but I don't exactly get witchy vibes from her." Despite the awkward conversation, a smile breaks out on my face.

Alec returns my smile with one of his own. "Well, that's good, I guess. Sorry. It was ridiculous of me to even bring up. It's not like people think she's an actual cauldron-and-boil type of witch. I think they just mean... spiritually." He frowns. "I hope I didn't offend you."

I can't stop watching the way his mouth moves so perfectly, paired with his wide and wondrous green eyes. I feel dizzy just standing with him. "I told you, that's not possible. Now, if we actually became friends, this would be an entirely different conversation."

The wattage of Alec's grin lights up his face. Finally, the tension vanishes, and his hand shoots out toward mine. "Alec Stone. We forgot this part yesterday."

I let out a breath, relieved that the uncomfortable conversation is over. My smile is unstoppable. "Katrina Summer. You can call me Kat, though."

We shake, and I can't help but stare down at the way his hand embraces mine. The strength in his hold is both warm and firm, connecting us in a way that makes me never want to let go.

He stands up straighter, a gleam sparkling in his eyes. "Okay, then. Kat, it is." He tilts his head. "You know, until recently, I didn't know Rose had a granddaughter."

This should probably upset me, but it doesn't. "Well, now you know." I probably shouldn't say what comes out of my mouth next, but it's out before I can stop it. "We were never close."

"So why now? Why live with your grandmother in this boring tiny town?"

I know he doesn't understand what he's asking me, so I try not to get emotional with him. "She's the only family I have. When my mom died, Rose was the one who took me in."

His apology is evident on his face. "I'm so sorry. I knew about your mom. I just didn't think... I'm sorry to hear about what happened."

"Thank you." I smile, wanting nothing more than to change the subject. "I don't think Apollo Beach is boring at all. It's smaller than Spring Lake in North Carolina. That's where I moved here from. And they definitely didn't have anything this"—I make a sweeping gesture while looking around—"charming."

Alec doesn't miss a beat. "I just moved here a little over a year ago myself. My dad got a job offer with the private college on the island, so I'm no stranger to being the new kid. We should stick together, you and me. I'll have your back; you have mine. You know?"

I nod, though I'm so caught off guard by his offer, and my voice gets stuck in my throat. I can't help but wonder why he's being so nice to me. No one ever took the time to get to know me back home. Then a dark, ugly feeling snakes through me when I remember how nice Steve was to me at first too. It's only a matter of time before something goes wrong here. Alec won't want to be my friend then. No one will.

"You said you were headed somewhere." He searches my gaze like he has a million more questions. "I would hate to make you late. Can I walk you out?"

I swallow my dark thoughts and push out a smile. "Sure."

We ride the elevator and exit on the bottom floor so I can check out my books at the front desk while Alec tells me about his Fourth of July party. "I know it's a long way off from now, but you have to come. We take over the beach. All the homes take part in the fun. And at the end of the night, we shoot off an insane fireworks show. Seriously, you have to be there."

We've just walked down the front steps of the library when he finishes his pitch, and I laugh. "I don't even know if I'll still be around by then. But if I'm here, I'll try to make it."

Alec frowns, the disappointment on his face boomeranging me straight in the gut. "What do you mean? You just got here."

It feels so strange to talk about this out loud, to someone I've just met, no less. "I know, but this isn't my home. Rose was nice to offer me a room, but I'll be eighteen soon. I can't impose on her forever."

He opens his mouth to speak again, but a shrill voice startles us both.

"Alec, we found you."

Dread weighs down my stomach when I see the two girls

who almost ran me over in their sports car earlier come bouncing up beside Alec. To make things worse, the driver presses right up against Alec's side.

My heart sinks when I realize he has a girlfriend. And not just any girlfriend. She's gorgeous. Tall and blond, she has deep-chocolate-brown eyes and legs for days. She slings an arm over Alec's shoulder, peers back at me with a glare, then looks at him with an amused expression. "Who's your new friend?"

Alec looks between us and shifts his body, creating an awkward space between him and the girl. "This is Kat, Rose Summer's granddaughter."

The looks on the girls' faces gives me the distinct impression they aren't surprised in the least. The shorter girl, who has light-brown hair, makes a face. "So the rumors are true. Rose has a granddaughter."

The blonde ignores her friend and asks me pointedly, "So, how long are you in town for?"

A heavy silence fills the air as I consider my response. "When I figure that out, I'll make sure to let you know."

After a pause, the blonde flashes a smile that resembles a smirk. "Well, then welcome to Apollo Beach. I'm Iris. This is Ava. Oh, and sorry about earlier." Iris exaggerates her pout. "I honestly didn't see you there. You should try using the crosswalk next time."

Ava pushes out a smile, mimicking Iris. "You really should be more careful, but..." Her eyes scan me from head to toe. "No harm done I see."

A sick feeling swirls in my stomach in response to her

condescending tone, but I force a smile onto my face. "No harm done at all."

Alec is looking between us. "What happened earlier? What am I missing?"

Iris lets out a haughty laugh and waves a hand in the air. "Nothing. So, anyway, Kat, welcome to town. If you ever need anything, Ava and I will be happy to help you. We've lived here our whole lives and know everything about the community. And Ava's father is the town sheriff."

I get a glimpse of Alec as Iris speaks. The way he keeps shifting away from the girls tells me I might have had it wrong. Maybe he and Iris aren't an item. Maybe they're just friends. Or maybe that's just wishful thinking. Just when that thought crosses my mind, Alec's eyes catch mine, and he gives me a sympathetic smile.

Iris must see the exchange because her fake smile narrows into a glare for a split second. Then she turns to Alec and perks right back up. "You ready to eat, babe?"

Babe? My stomach drops again.

Alec sighs, nods, then lifts his eyebrows at me. "Do you want to join us? We're just grabbing some lunch."

I shake my head. "Thanks, but I'm meeting up with Charlotte."

Alec flashes me a final smile, his gaze lingering on mine for a few seconds longer. "See you around, Kat."

My smile falters when I realize he's not the last of them to look away. My eyes catch on Iris, her lids narrowing into daggers aimed straight for me. Then with a quick toss of her hair, she whips her head around and links arms with Alec—a possessive move if I ever saw one.

As I watch the three of them walk off toward the parking lot, there's a sinking feeling in my gut. I may not be planning to stay in Apollo Beach for long, but it's people like Iris and Ava who remind me why I planned to maintain a low profile while I'm here. I'll get a job, save some money, keep to myself, and then maybe—just maybe—I'll escape this town without throwing anyone else out of a window.

EIGHT

I walk through the parking lot of Island Grille and meet Charlotte inside the front doors to wait for our seats. The bay-front restaurant is a circular building with pillars surrounding it, reminding me of a temple, with faux crumbling, gold-capped columns, but the seating areas, inside and out, have more of an island oasis feel. The inside bar especially has more of a tiki vibe than anything else.

We're so close to the water that the breeze blows freely through the open spaces. The outer tables, which face the bay front, are decorated with white and navy umbrellas. There's a circular bar on one end of the room, with TV screens placed throughout. Beer and alcohol brands are posted all over the walls of the bar, and tattered nautical items are scattered on the supporting wood pillars. Looking around more, I see pool tables, dartboards, a Ping-Pong table, and even a stack of board games on the opposite side of the room.

The hostess smiles at us, her curious eyes lingering on me before she turns to Charlotte. "Hey, Charlotte. You want your usual spot in the back?"

Charlotte shakes her head. "Not today, Trisha. This is Kat's first time here. Do you have a water-view available?"

Trisha flashes a bright smile at me then looks down at her sheet before marking something off. "For you two, I can make something available." She winks, grabs a couple of menus, then gestures for us to follow her.

The bounce in her step makes her long, curly blond hair sway in her ponytail. She looks to be my age, and I can't help but wonder if she knows Alec, Iris, and Ava. This town seems to be small enough for everyone to know everyone else.

My wandering eyes spot the happy threesome already sitting in the section where we're headed. *Speak of the devils.*

Alec's back faces me, but Iris sees me. I smile and raise my arm in a wave, just to be friendly, and am rewarded with a smirk. She looks away and continues her conversation.

Rude. It's like that girl had me pegged as an enemy since the moment she spotted me on the beach. Was it something I did? Was it the attention of Alec? Either way, it just feels like the beginning of everything I dealt with back home. I can't go through that again.

"So, what did you get at the library?" Charlotte's eyes are already on the books.

Discomfort shakes through me. I don't know why. Maybe because of what Alec mentioned about Wicca. "Just a few books." I run my hand along the top cover. "Something about being here makes me want to understand more about my heritage, I guess. You mentioned something about the summer solstice, so I figured I could start there." I sit up straighter, remembering something. "And there's a statue of a woman in the library, right in the center on the bottom floor. The librarian there said no one knew who the woman was. Do you?"

Charlotte rests her hands on the table and leans in slightly. "Yes, I do. Her name is Astina Summer."

I let out a laugh. "Summer? It's not enough that my grandparents named an island and a housing development after themselves, but they had to take it a step further and name a statue after themselves too?"

Charlotte bites down on her lip appearing amused. "They didn't name the statue after themselves, Kat. What on earth makes you think that?"

I squint at her, trying to determine just how delusional this woman is. "The librarian said the woman was some sort of goddess from ancient Greece." I stifle another laugh that bubbles over my discomfort.

"Astina is an ancestor of yours from thousands of years ago, and that statue is as old as she is. It's quite remarkable that it's still standing."

My eyes widen when I realize Charlotte completely believes what she's telling me. "What makes her so important that she gets a statue? I've never even heard of her."

Charlotte presses her lips together like she's trying to keep from laughing again. "She's quite important to your lineage. I wouldn't be so quick to brush her off."

"Why do you think I'm asking you about her? I want to understand."

I expect Charlotte to scold me for my growing impatience and frustration, but her expression only softens.

"Astina's existence is a mystery, and is rumored to have come about rather spontaneously, much like that of other primordial gods."

I have to bite down on my lip to keep from bursting out with a laugh. "Interesting."

Charlotte tilts her head at me and rolls her eyes. "I can see you're taking this seriously."

Heat swarms my chest. "You expect me to believe all of this? You're talking about immaculate conception."

Charlotte chuckles. "I suppose I am. I thought you said you wanted to understand."

I scoff. "I was just asking about the importance of a statue."

Charlotte nods. "Perhaps Rose can elaborate for you when you speak with her." She pushes her chair back. "I'm heading to the restroom. Be right back. Order an appetizer if you like."

As she walks off, I look down at the menu angrily. There are times when I'm so in awe of this town, I can barely keep my jaw shut. Then there are times like now, when I wonder why I ever came here. Surely, I could have let the state place me somewhere until I turned eighteen. But then what? My mom had nothing but debt and bills she could barely pay. I would have been homeless. And without any education or employment references, who knows if I would have found a job? Coming here felt like my only real choice at the time, but I'm really starting to question that decision.

A figure approaches. I notice his black shoes first, his tanned muscular legs next, then his black shorts. The sleeves of his black button-down dress shirt are rolled and pushed up his arms. *It's him.*

A shiver shakes through me as I make the connection before I even look up to see his face. Up close, he's even more intimidating than he was last night when he glared at me from beneath his cap. He's got to be over six feet tall, with bold blue eyes and scruff around his jaw. If I had to guess, I would think he was somewhere in his midtwenties, but I don't know why I'm thinking that hard about it. That's when I notice something I somehow missed the first couple of times I saw him. A jagged scar extends from just below his brow to his cheek.

His intense stare narrows as he just stands there and says nothing while holding a notepad and a pen poised in his hand. "Well, are you going to order or what?" His gruff voice is even darker than his glare.

What is this guy's problem? He glares as if he hates me, but he doesn't even know me.

My mouth opens, but I can't seem to find the words. Even if I could, I'm not sure I'll be able to utter a single thing with my heart in my throat. I want to ask him if he his problem is with me or just life in general. It's not like he took one look at me staring at him through the passenger window then decided to hate me. Maybe he was having a bad night, and I just happened to drive by at the wrong time.

I look down at the menu, trying to buy some time to work up the nerve to look up at him again, but not even a second passes before he turns and walks away. My eyes snap up just as he stops at the next table over and tosses me yet another glare. This time, I don't shy away. I narrow my eyes back in his direction before averting them completely.

"That Kat girl is so weird."

I jerk my head to find the origin of the voice, but it sounds more like a whisper all around me. I swivel my head until my eyes catch on Iris. She's currently leaning forward and talking to her friends while darting glances at me. But she's several tables away. There's no way it could have been her speaking.

I whip my head in all directions, expecting to find the true culprit. Then I hear more whispers. This time, the voice belongs to a male.

"No, she's not. She's nice. Give her a break."

My head turns back to face the threesome.

"Of course you think she's nice. You think everyone is nice."

I'm no lip reader, but the words match the movement of Iris's mouth. My heart starts to pound.

"And that's a bad thing how?"

"She clearly likes you," Ava chimes in.

"What? Why would you think that?"

"Alec, you are so funny. The girl obviously has a crush on you. You don't want her to get the wrong idea, do you?"

If I needed confirmation that I can actually hear their conversation, then I have it now. Iris just said his name, and now he's reacting.

"Back off of her, you guys. She's new. She's perfectly nice. And she's a freaking Summer, for heaven's sake. She's practically royalty here."

Iris and Ava don't waste a breath before they're howling in a fit of giggles. Even then, hope sparks in my chest at the fact that he's sticking up for me. No one ever sticks up for me.

Alec rolls his eyes when the girls' laughter lingers. "Whatever. I invited her to my Fourth of July party so she can meet everyone. You two should try to get to know her."

When the girls expel their last laugh and wipe the tears from their eyes, Iris is shaking her head. "C'mon, Alec. Are you forgetting everything I told you about the Summers?"

"You mean about them being witches? That's ridiculous."

Iris glares. "There's something strange about that family. Especially Rose. And the fact that it took Kat's mom to die for her to come back here. What's up with that anyway? She never even came to visit."

"That's none of our business," Alec snaps.

Ava chimes in, matching Iris's venomous tone, quietly but matter-of-factly, "Rose won't always rule this town, you know? She's old. Others more suitable are ready to step up, and soon, they will."

Iris nods. "That's right. And when that happens, you won't want anything to do with Katrina Summer."

Another chill courses through my veins as I reel back from the conversation. This isn't just a friendly exchange between friends. This goes deeper. They're talking about my grandmother and her rightful place in Apollo Beach. How dare they? Why do they feel so possessive of this town? What does any of it even matter to them, anyway?

"Kat." Charlotte's voice snaps me out of my trance, and I

look up to see her sitting in the booth, a worried look on her face. "You okay?"

I perk up quickly. "Yeah, I just thought I heard something." I shake my head and laugh, not wanting to clue her in to what I just heard. I start awkwardly thumbing through the menu. "So, what's good to eat here?"

The way her silence lingers makes me wonder if she knows exactly what I just heard, but then she's back to her happy self. "The Summer salad is great. So are the burgers. Honestly, you can't go wrong. What are you in the mood for?"

My eyes are pinned on the burger section, reading the description of each item while my mouth waters.

"Are you ready to order, or should I come back again?"

The gruff voice has an instant effect on my heart, causing it to triple its beat. I raise an eyebrow at his tone, refusing to meet his gaze again. Someone should tell this asshole that his impatient demeanor is unbecoming. Not that it would do much. Something tells me he wouldn't care at all.

"I'll have a chicken salad wrap with fries," Charlotte says. "Kat? Did you decide?"

I hand the menu to the giant grump creating a shadow where the sun should be, then I look up, matching his chilly gaze. "I'll try the temple burger. No onions or pickles, please. Oh, and extra lettuce if you can."

His jaw ticks. "Sure thing. How would you like that cooked? Rare, medium rare...?" He doesn't finish his sentence, but I suspect he's trying to offend me with his strange question.

I do my best to stuff my annoyance deep into my chest. "Medium well will do."

"And for your side?" he asks dryly.

I'm not even sure what my choices are. "I'll have a side salad if that's an option."

He doesn't confirm my choice. "Is that all? Perhaps you'd like to try our crème brûlée as well?"

My chest heats, and my jaw drops at his patronizing tone. Who does this guy think he is? I snap my mouth shut and adopt a syrupy-sweet smile. "Only if it's on the house."

He yanks the menu from my grip, obviously annoyed. "It's not." He starts to walk away.

"Oh," Charlotte adds, making him halt. "Do you mind bringing us some waters too? Extra ice. Extra tall glasses."

The guy looks between us both like he knows he's been caught being a prick, and in that split-second when he's not looking at me, I search quickly for a name tag like the one I saw Trisha wearing. Nothing. Not that I should be surprised. The guy clearly goes out of his way to be a rebel.

I watch the grump walk away before I look over to find Charlotte's waiting eyes and an amused smile on her face.

"What?" I ask.

She lets out a laugh and raises her brows. "Do you want me to spell it out for you, Katrina? You have a crush."

I can feel a blush creeping up my neck. "On that guy? No way. He's not very nice."

"Maybe not, but I could feel you overheating from here. I couldn't figure out if you were going to kiss him or lose your temper. Neither would have been a great option." She leans in with warning in her eyes. "I know about how things were for you back in Silver Lake. You were misunderstood. The kids were vile. And you didn't know how to control that temper of yours. I can teach you."

I swallow, confused and intrigued in equal measure. "What? Is there a school file on me or something? Because the things they think I did... didn't happen the way they said they did."

Charlotte nods. "I trust that you're correct. Even still, there are things you can do to protect yourself."

I frown. "So you think I did those things? You think I pushed Steve out of a window?" Just talking about the events from back in Silver Lake makes me want to cry. I look up to find the grump's accusing eyes pinned on me. I didn't think I was talking *that* loud. I'm quick to turn my gaze away. "I didn't touch him," I say in a quieter voice.

Charlotte nods again. "Of course you didn't. But there are moments when our emotions can get the better of us. Sometimes, it's not what we do or don't do, but how we react. There's a power within all of us, Kat. For people like you and me, that power can become so intense, it feels like we might implode. Am I right?"

I can feel my bones shaking with her words. Somehow, Charlotte just explained it perfectly. "Yes." It's just a whisper, but I can tell by her slow inhale that she heard it.

"You can learn to control that energy, Kat. I can help you."

"How?"

Charlotte smiles, altering the mood from intense to relaxed in one single beat. "For starters, you can change your mindset. It's you who chooses the energy you accept and release, not the other way around. You should only take in what you know you can control."

I think about her words. The concept seems so simple, but I have no idea where to start when it comes to applying the thought process to myself. So when the grump returns to drop off our ice waters, I flash him the biggest smile I can muster and say, "Thank you," as if there's never been a problem at all. "You don't happen to be hiring, do you?" I bat my eyes up at him.

When shock registers on his face, I want to laugh.

"Um, no. We're not." That's all he gives me before he's walking away again.

Trisha must have overheard him as she's walking by, because she twists her face up at his back and stops at our table. "Don't mind Johnny. He's always like that. Most of us just ignore him. We actually are hiring." Her blue eyes sparkle with the sun at her back. "Do you want me to get you an application?"

I flash her an appreciative smile. "I would love one, but —" I chew on my bottom lip as my insecurities rise to the surface. "I don't have any work experience or anything."

Trisha shrugs. "We all have to start somewhere." Then she sticks out her hand. "I'm Trisha, by the way."

We shake. "I'm Kat."

"Welcome to Apollo Beach, Kat. You should call me if you ever get stir-crazy. It's a small town, but there's plenty to do. I'd be happy to be your guide, anytime."

My chest warms. "Thank you."

Charlotte reaches out and squeezes the girl's arm. "I'm sure Kat would love that. Thank you, Trisha."

"No problem. Let me go grab you that application."

She hurries off, and I'm already feeling a hundred times better than I was minutes ago. Between broody Johnny and the catty crew a few tables over, I was sure my stay here was going downhill fast. But maybe I actually stand a chance of surviving this place for the short term.

NINE

Night passes without another vision or dream to wake me in a cold sweat. I expected the dreams to come. In a strange way, I wanted them to come. As haunting as they are, I can't help but feel like they're trying to tell me something important. Maybe the dreams are a warning. Or maybe they're telling me the opposite—that I'll find happiness in this small town.

Alec's face crosses my mind, and I wave it away, knowing those thoughts are only distractions. There's no point in getting comfortable here, not when I'm planning to leave in a month. It's a good thing too. If the confrontation with Ava and Iris is any indication of what I can expect, then I don't want it.

An image of Trisha pops into my mind next, as if my subconscious wants to remind me that not everyone here is a complete asshole. She handed me that job application like she wanted me to return it too. I promised her I would while simultaneously ignoring the glare Johnny shot me from the other side of the room. The rebel in me wants the job even more now that I know it would bother him.

I'm still thinking about the events from yesterday when I'm at breakfast with Rose.

She's already finished with her meal, and now she's watching me push food around my plate. "How was your shopping trip yesterday?"

"Good. I picked out a dress for the party. I promise to repay you."

"Don't be foolish. You don't need to repay me." Rose's insistent tone tells me she's not up for arguing.

Sighing, I look up at her. "Okay, but I'm still going to get a job."

Rose nods. "I can see that it's important to you. I saw the application for Island Grille. I can put in a good word with the manager."

Anger flares in my chest. I hate that this is my reaction, and I'm not exactly sure where it comes from exactly. But I don't want any of Rose's handouts. "I'd like to try to get the job on my own, if that's okay."

Rose looks slightly taken aback, but she nods. "Okay, dear. Then I wish you all the luck in the world."

"Thank you."

Her face relaxes into a smile, and her shoulders seem to fall slightly too. "Of course," she starts, catching me off guard. "You'll be busy soon with... other things, so perhaps you should hold off on submitting that application for now."

"What? Why?"

Rose shrugs. "You'll see."

There it is again. The secrets. The mystery. The deep sense that there's a bigger plan for me. Anger sweeps through me again. "I don't understand. What is it that you think I'll be busy with?"

A small smile pushes up her cheeks. "Oh, all sorts of things."

I force my next breath to be a slow one as I try to steady the rush of heat swirling through me. That's it. I can't wait to tell her anymore. Rose thinks I have a future in this place, when the opposite is true. While I feel like I owe her nothing, my conscience tells me differently. "I plan to leave after my eighteenth birthday."

Rose gasps. "What? You most certainly will not."

I ignore her and continue. "While I appreciate you taking me in and giving me a home and food and clothes, I will not overstay my welcome."

"Overstay your welcome? But this is your home, Katrina. You must stay." She leans forward, her expressive eyes firm on me.

"No offense, Rose, but we haven't had a relationship my entire life, and now you want me to make this my permanent home? I can't. I won't."

"You must."

"Why?" I demand. "And don't give me a vague answer and tell me I'll understand in time, because I want to understand right now. Why must I stay?"

"Because this is your home. It's where your parents met. It's where you were born. You belong here, Katrina."

My jaw drops. "I don't know where I belong, but it's not here."

"It is." Her tone is firm, almost scolding. "I understand

your frustration, but this isn't something I can elaborate on at this moment."

"Why not?" I laugh incredulously.

Rose sighs. "There are discoveries you must make on your own. Here is what I can say. There is a circle of life that began at the root of our ancestry, and on the day of your eighteenth birthday, you'll no longer be able to deny it anymore."

"The root of our ancestry?" Somehow, I feel like the words are important. I'm racking my brain when the statue from Apollo Beach Library comes to mind. "Astina Summer."

Rose frowns. "Where did you hear that name?"

The last thing I want to do is drag Charlotte into this. She was only trying to help. "I asked around after I saw her statue at the library. She's beautiful."

Rose nods. "The most beautiful goddess of all time."

"What kind of goddess is she?"

"The Goddess of Enchantment."

I shake my head, confused. "I thought Circe was the Goddess of Enchantment."

Rose's brows lift. "Circe is the Goddess of Enchant*ments*. A big difference in our world. Astina, however she came to be, was born on the summer solstice."

Something triggers my memory of the conversation Alec and I had yesterday. "So, what? Was she a Wiccan or something?"

Rose glares, her nostrils flaring. "Absolutely not. Where would you get such an idea?"

I sigh, frustrated with how hard these dots are to

connect. "All this talk of the solstice and how obsessed you are with your culture—I'm just trying to understand. I went to the library yesterday to find some books to try and understand what the big deal is. Did you know that there are people in this town who believe you're a Wiccan?"

Rose takes a few seconds to answer, like she's trying to find the right words. "Do I know the things people say behind my back? Yes, I am quite aware. Do I care? No. Am I a Wiccan? No. Not that there's anything wrong with it. That's simply a tired rumor that I wish you would not involve yourself in."

Just hearing her say all of that makes me feel a million times better. I don't expect her to elaborate.

Rose stands from the table. "There's something I need to show you. I was planning to show you after your birthday, but I think you are ready now."

I follow her reluctantly, hating that we blew over the fact that I have no intention of staying in town much longer. We pass through the house, and she leads me down the narrow hallway that Charlotte referred to as "Rose's quarters."

She stops halfway down the hall, where she pushes open a door to reveal a spacious, two-story room bursting with light. A library. It's much smaller than the one I visited yesterday, but somehow much grander in beauty. Its cream shelves with gold trim and black spiral staircases on each side of the room give off a whimsical air that goes unmatched. I'm in awe as I pivot slowly to take it all in.

In front of the massive bay window facing the water is a living room setup. The domed ceiling is made entirely of glass, through which the morning sunlight shines in. The rest of the room is filled with rows upon rows of books.

I breathe deeply.

"This is the Summer library," Rose says. "Your grandfather spent the majority of his time here." She watches my face for a second before continuing. "You'll find more information about our heritage here than in any public library can offer."

I swallow, my fingers itching to touch the spines. "Okay."

Rose gestures for me to follow her to a section of shelves. "Most of these are first editions. Some are just for entertainment, but most have been passed down from our ancestors. Some are even handwritten and very well preserved. Any information you seek on our heritage will be here, and maybe then you'll understand why your birthday is such a special day."

I'm still looking around in awe. "Thank you for showing me this. It's incredible."

Rose makes an appreciative noise. "I'm glad you like it. I hope you'll spend time here. It has only seen dust since your grandfather passed."

I nod, noting silently that there isn't a speck of dust in the room from what I can see. "Thank you. But what does any of this have to do with why people connect the solstice to witchcraft?"

Rose looks as if she's pondering her words carefully. "Well, dear, Wiccans practice the art of magic. They worship the earth, the gods, and goddesses. They sacrifice things to stay holy to their gods. The difference, however, is simple.

Our family—the Summers—we merely come from the magic they worship."

I let out an incredulous laugh, unable to help myself. "What?"

"Let me try that again." I can tell Rose is struggling with her own vagueness. "We don't practice any art, for we are that art."

I glare at her, unappreciative of her joke. "The art of magic?"

Rose nods. "That's right. Wiccans believe in the four elements—you know, earth, wind, fire, and water. They believe in the gods who supposedly control the elements like alchemy. It's just a way of life. And Wiccans believe the summer solstice is celebrated as a day to give themselves to their greater beings through sacrifice. To us, the solstice is a time when we celebrate all nature has to offer."

"So then, it's more spiritual than anything. It's not... witchcraft." I let out an uncomfortable laugh, waiting for Rose to agree.

Instead, she turns away like what she just said was completely normal. "Have fun exploring, dear. I think I'll turn in for a nap now. Let Charlotte know when you're done, and she can take you anywhere you'd like to go."

"Rose," I call.

Perhaps it's the desperation in my tone, but she stops in her tracks and turns to face me. "What is it, Katrina?"

"Something weird is going on with me. Why do I think you might know why that is?"

Rose frowns. "Weird how?"

I tell her about my strange vision on the beach and my

nightmare of the woman who looked like me in the mirror. I explain how Iris nearly killed me with her car, then I was somehow able to hear her conversation at Island Grille. "Why do I feel like all of this is connected?"

Rose nods slowly. "Because it is, dear. Everything is connected. Always. But I assure you, everything you're going through is normal and nothing to be alarmed about. You're in a new home and a new town, and information can be... overwhelming. As for the conversation you overheard, running a small town like this comes with a certain responsibility. Unfortunately, politics gets involved, and certain folks feel a sense of privilege because they've lived here all their lives. Most of us in the community are in agreement with the laws we've established. The majority want me as their leader, but there are some who don't." Rose shrugs.

As Rose speaks, I can see a sadness in her eyes. "I don't understand. What is it that they want?"

She sighs. "It's complicated. Some of them want to rip down trees and bulldoze historical landmarks to build popular chain restaurants and hotels so they can promote Summer Island as a tourism spot. It would destroy everything our family has spent our lives trying to preserve."

"Why would they want to do that? What's in it for them?"

Rose doesn't even bat an eye before she answers. "Power. Greed. There's a darkness in this world that feeds the weak. It's my job to keep those people in check." She winks at me then gestures around the room. "I can see your curiosity will suit this room just fine."

There's a soft click of the door as she exits the room, and I'm left alone with my swirling thoughts and endless list of questions that only seems to be growing. Rose says it's all connected—my dreams, my vision, and my magnified senses and strength. My eyes scan the endless shelves of books. Somehow, I'm to find my answers here.

Guess I better get started.

TEN

Summer Library is quickly becoming my favorite room in the house. Some days, I spend my afternoons scanning the wood-paneled bookcases. On others, I just sit beneath the dome ceiling and bask in the sunlight.

The collection of books is filled with classic literature, like the works of Shakespeare, Fitzgerald, and Joyce, and the list goes on and on. But the majority of the books revolve around Greek mythology, which is what I spend most of my time devouring. Every story I read is either an interpretation or reinterpretation of other stories, but with each one, I learn something new.

I get a little stir-crazy five days later and ask Charlotte to drive me to the island so I can drop off my job application at Island Grille. She's more than happy to oblige, and she waits in the car while I head inside.

"Summer, you say?" Roy, the manager of Island Grille, is gawking as if I've just cursed at him. "I suppose I have no choice then. The old woman send you here?" His voice is deep and agitated, but I get the distinct impression he doesn't dislike my grandmother. He may even be fond of her.

My eyes flash with determination. I don't want to rely on the Summer name to gain work. "Rose didn't send me here. Trisha told me that you might be hiring."

Roy tilts his head and folds his arms across his chest. "Is that right?" His eyes scan my face as if performing a lie detector test. After a moment he releases his stance and smiles. His teeth are big and white, clearly false. "Well, just because you're Rose's granddaughter doesn't mean I'm gonna hire you just like that. We're the busiest restaurant in Apollo Beach, young lady, and I need talented wait staff helping keep this place afloat."

"I am talented," I say, discomforted by his assertion. I stand up straighter, placing my fists upon my hips.

"Oh yeah?" His eyes crinkle with amusement. "How so? Have you ever worked before?"

So maybe I've never worked a day in my life, but I'm not about to let him think that matters. "I have great balance. I can carry a tray. I have a picture perfect memory, so I won't forget an order, and I'm fast. Your cooks will have to keep up with me."

Roy looks down at my application, bobbing his head as his eyes scan it. "Well, you're underage, so you can't work the bar. The only place I can put you is here on the main floor. Busiest floor around. You'll be waiting on six to eight tables at a time on the weekends. You think you can handle that?"

His challenge causes me to raise an eyebrow. "Of course I can."

He smirks. "Is that right, pretty lady? Well, we'll see.

You'll need to audition. Monday night. If you make the cut, I'll keep ya. If you drop a dish, forget an order, or piss anyone off, you're out of here."

I'm having trouble making out whether to be intimidated by Roy or not. He seems well-meaning, harmless even, but his gruffness throws me.

Before I have a chance to ask Roy how he wants me to dress, I'm distracted by a figure that appears at the entrance. It's Johnny, wearing his signature black attire.

Great. Roy just said I don't stand a chance if I piss anyone off. Seems all I have to do is be present to anger the grumpy bartender. I quickly scan Johnny's face for any sign that his feelings about me might have changed. My eyes fix on the jagged scar below his brow then flicker to his perfect nose and finally to his ice-cold blue eyes. When I catch him staring back at me with an earth-shaking intensity, warmth spreads up my neck.

Johnny's eyes move toward Roy, probably assessing the situation. When he looks back at me, his expression dims.

"Hey, Johnny." Roy calls him over, and I immediately tense, locking my knees together to help steady myself for whatever the firing squad shoots my way.

Johnny saunters over without taking his eyes off me. I feel weak and insignificant compared to the guy now standing tall in front of me. I'm freed from his spell when he turns his eyes to Roy.

"Johnny Pierce, meet Katrina Sum—"

"Kat," I interrupt.

They both turn to stare at me as if I've soured their milk.

I take an automatic step back. My eyes move from one grump to the next. "It's just Kat."

Roy rolls his eyes and turns back to Johnny. "Just Kat over here wants a job. I'm auditioning her for a waitress spot. We need the help. Show her around, will you? And I'll need you to train her on Monday."

"You mean you want me to babysit?" Johnny practically spits the words out.

Every fiber in my body is on alert, and my mouth falls open. "Excuse me," I say, my eyes narrowed. "I don't need a sitter. I can handle myself just fine."

Johnny's gaze pierces mine. He obviously disagrees.

Seemingly in a rush to brush over the tension in the air, Roy says, "Just show her around. I'm going to be busy prepping the permits for the carnival, so we can use the extra help."

Carnival?

He shoots a final look at Johnny. "Be nice." With that, Roy stalks off, leaving Johnny and me standing here. Alone.

Johnny watches me, evaluating my features like he's picking every inch of me apart. I start to wonder if his dislike for me has something to do with Rose. Or maybe he's friends with Iris and Ava. There does seem to be an entire I Hate Katrina Summer Club I don't know about. But even while I'm considering it, I know it's a stretch. Johnny appears much older than Alec and the girls. He doesn't seem like someone who would hang out with that crowd.

"I thought I told you we weren't hiring."

I glare. "Yeah, well, you lied. So here I am."

The tension between us is exhausting. He glares down at

me, eyes transparent, expressing his distaste for me. I shift my stance. I'm used to being bullied and made fun of, but not this. He stares at me like a hungry lion ready to pounce on his prey.

If he wants me to cower, it doesn't work. I am, however, annoyed. "You don't have to give me a tour. I can find my own way." I step to the side, but he steps out, too, blocking my path.

I'm careful to avoid his eyes as he speaks.

"Come with me." His gruff tone is a shock to my center. He steps out of my way and moves toward the double doors that lead to the kitchen. I rush to keep up.

I could ask him what his problem is with me, but I choose a different tactic. "I'm sorry for whatever it is I've done to you to make you hate me."

Although he's in front of me, I notice his expression soften. Or maybe it's my imagination.

"I'll show you the kitchen before I start my shift."

He's silent the entire way to the kitchen, but he's nice enough to open the wooden swinging doors for me to walk through. I take this opportunity to offer him my friendliest smile, hoping we've moved past the awkward portion of our working relationship. He grazes my eyes before looking forward into the kitchen. No such luck.

"Hey, Mikey," Johnny calls out to the stout chef with grease stains smeared over his white shirt. I can't help but notice that Johnny greets him with a fake Jersey accent. I'm confused. His expression appears playful. Johnny doesn't seem like someone who makes jokes, but maybe he just doesn't make jokes with me.

Mikey stands behind the counter with a grin on his face and two knives raised in greeting. "Johnny," he calls back in the same accent, and I realize it's a thing they have together. "Who's the pretty lady?" Mikey calls out now, his eyes returning to whatever he's cutting.

I blush as Johnny points a lazy finger in my direction. "This is Kat, Rose Summer's granddaughter. She's going to work here."

"I just got an audition actually." As soon as I say the words, I regret them.

Johnny's eyes jerk to mine, and his playfulness is gone. "What's it with you correcting everyone?" His eyes reveal his annoyance.

I inhale slowly through my nose, bite my tongue, and sink back to listen to his instructions.

"We put the tickets for the orders here." He points to a circular device on the edge of the metal workstation. "They'll set the food up on the edge when it's ready, and then you take the completed order to your table."

As Johnny walks around the kitchen, naming everything and telling me what it does, I reconsider my decision to work here. It's not like me to give up, but why would I choose to work with someone who hates me for no apparent reason? This was his territory first, and whatever his problem is doesn't seem to be getting better. Surely there's another job available on the island.

He walks me to the back corner of the kitchen to show me where the refreshments and silverware are kept. I stop him there. "Thank you for the tour, Johnny. I don't think I'll take the audition, though."

He blinks as if puzzled by my sudden decision. Making him momentarily speechless provides me with an inkling of joy, but it doesn't last.

"Why are you telling me this? You need to tell Roy." He leads me to the opposite side of the room, where two doors read Office and Break Room.

The door to the break room swings open, and Trisha stands there with a bright smile. I beam back at her in recognition, happy to see a friendly face.

"Kat! What are you doing back here?" Trisha's long bouncy blond hair sits high on her head in a ponytail. Her blue eyes twinkle.

"I was applying for that job, but"—I throw a glance at Johnny—"I don't think it's the right place for me."

Trisha frowns. "No! I need you. There aren't any other girls my age here."

Johnny sighs loudly and shuffles his feet, most likely irritated at our brief detour from my exit. We ignore him.

"Roy will hire you," Trisha says, trying to convince me. "We're desperate for help."

In an abrupt move, Johnny brushes past me, and all my tiny arm hairs rise in full salute. "I've got to clock in for my shift. I'll see you on Monday." He doesn't spend a second more with me before escaping through the break room door.

Trisha scrunches her face in response to his rude exit, then she grins. "I'm so happy you'll be working here with me. Between Roy and Johnny, I was going mad surrounded by so much testosterone."

"No kidding. Are they like that all the time?"

Trisha shrugs. "Yes, but Johnny keeps to himself mostly.

Too bad, right? He's a grump, but he's a hot grump." She winks at me as if she might have a thing for him. "And Roy is really an old teddy bear once you get to know him. You'll see."

I smile at her, thankful for her encouraging words. "Sounds like you've worked here for a while."

"Since I was sixteen. It's a great job. Great location. Awesome tips. Flexible schedule. I'm going to need it since I'm hopefully starting college in the fall."

I light up since it's obviously something that makes her happy. "Hopefully?"

Trisha cringes. "I have my heart set on the School of Gaia here on the island. I've been wait-listed."

Seeing her disappointment makes my heart squeeze. But I'm also confused since Rose gave me the impression that I could get in easily. "Well, I'm sure you'll get in. When do you hear?"

She shrugs. "Anytime between now and the end of the summer." She sighs then waves her hand in the air. "I thought I was a shoo-in since I've lived here my whole life, but you never know who's going to make it in. They don't go by grades or extracurriculars like most schools."

I scrunch my face, confused. "Then what do they go by?"

Trisha laughs and shakes her head. "No one really knows. Everyone from my graduating class who applied has already made it in, though, so it's kind of a bummer."

I tilt my head. "I'm sorry. I hope you get in."

"What are you planning to do next year? I know you just moved here, so it's probably too late for you to apply to the college." Her expression changes. "Oh, unless your grandma pulls some strings or something."

There's no way I'm telling Trisha what Rose told me. "I'm not sure if I'm even going to college." I push out a smile, hoping my confession makes her feel better. "I'm not even sure if I'm sticking around the entire summer. Rose wants me to but—"

Trisha's face falls. "Oh, Kat. You have to stay. I have good intuition about people, and I already like you."

Something about the girl seems so incredibly sincere that her words make my chest warm. "You do?"

She nods emphatically. "Yes. Which means you're stuck with me. Starting with this job. Do the audition. Okay?"

Just as I open my mouth to tell her I need to think about it, the door to the staff room opens.

"Excuse me." Johnny steps past us, and as he does I take in his crisp, woodsy scent. It reminds me of an ocean breeze blowing over a forest filled with tropical fruit. Whatever the concoction is sends a buzz through me I can't ignore. Damn him.

Trisha tugs on my arm and leans in to whisper, "Don't worry about Johnny. He'll warm up to you."

I can't help my laugh. "Somehow I doubt that."

As soon as the words are out of my mouth, I swear I see Johnny's back muscles tighten through his shirt. He doesn't linger for another second to make me think on it. Instead, he pushes through the double doors and into the restaurant.

ELEVEN

Charlotte summoned me to the great room for afternoon tea. So I dress up for the occasion in a simple blue sundress, gold sandals, and my gold charm bracelet. It's been days since I've seen Rose, and I'm curious what she wants to chat about.

"Sit, sit." Rose gestures for me to take a seat on the couch across from her. "How are you adjusting, Katrina?"

I contemplate how truthful my response should be. "I'm adjusting fine, I suppose. With all things considered."

"Yes, well, I don't doubt it's all a bit... unsettling. You lost your mother, and now you're expected to start over in a strange new place. Your grandfather's passing was the hardest thing I've ever gone through. He was my best friend, and then one day, he wasn't around anymore. Loss like that creates an emptiness inside of us that can never be replaced. I understand what you are going through now, and I just want you to know that I'm here for you."

Listening to her speak of my grandfather brings me sadness. "I'm very sorry to hear of your loss. Charlotte told me about the fire. My mom only spoke of how much she cared about him."

Rose's face relaxes into a smile. "Yes, your mother and George had a very special relationship. She sent flowers after his passing. I imagine his passing was hard for her." Rose tilts her head. "It makes me sad that you never knew your grandfather. He was an amazing man, a wonderful father, a giver to the community, and a natural-born leader. The best husband I could have ever wished for." Rose turns her head, deep in thought.

My curiosity gets the better of me. "How did the fire start?"

She bows her head, her eyes drifting over my shoulder and out the window. "There was no trace of how it started. George and I were out at the local market. We came home and saw the smoke. Of course that stubborn man had to run inside. He located the source of the fire inside the library. While he was trying to smother the flames, he got caught between some shelves."

"Charlotte told me it was you who pulled him out of there. You're a hero."

Rose lets out a laugh. "I'm no hero, dear. I was able to get him out of there alive that day, but the fire had already reached his lungs. A real hero would have known. Anyway, I was so sorry to hear about your mother, Katrina. You may find this hard to believe, but there was a time when we were very close. She was like a daughter to me. I raised her as if she were my own daughter, and I've never stopped loving her. When I heard of her passing, I was heartbroken."

A strange mix of emotions swirls through me. Confusion,

doubt, anger. "Forgive me, Rose, but if that's true, then why haven't I met you until now?"

Rose shakes her head and meets my gaze with a sorrowful expression. "I tried to keep a relationship with her, but she wanted nothing to do with George and me after your parents—well, things got complicated, I suppose."

I swallow. This is the closest I've come to speaking about my father in years. The pain of knowing he chose to never know me is as embarrassing as it is hurtful. "I don't think it sounds complicated at all. He got my mom pregnant and then didn't want the responsibility of fatherhood."

Silence stretches between us as Rose takes a slow sip of her tea. "Let's just say I understood her reasons for leaving, and I respected them." Rose sets her cup down and rests her hands on her lap. "I trust over time you'll come to understand it all too. Like we've already discussed, our family has a responsibility to this place. The moment she held you for the first time, all she wanted to do was protect you. She believed the only way that was possible was to cut off all ties with our family."

"But why? Protect me from what?"

Rose opens her mouth a few times before finally speaking. "Grace was afraid of a destiny that could not be altered. She ran from it, she tried to control it, and she sacrificed us with the belief that you would be better off." Rose takes a deep breath. "You would have ended up here no matter what, Katrina. Apollo Beach, Summer Island, this manor— this is your destiny. Not even your mother, with the best intentions in the world, had the power to stop that. Unfortunately, divine forces were at play. That's why you're here today."

Rose's cryptic answer causes a sudden wave of heat to shoot through my body. "You're telling me my mom is dead because of some divine intervention? Do you know how crazy that sounds?"

"I assure you, none of this is crazy. You just don't understand it all yet."

Her words only make me shake so hard there's a rattling between my ears. My emotions—my fear, anger, and pain—are so intense, it's like they're all snowballing downhill without an end in sight. It just builds and builds until I feel like I might explode. "How can I when there are so many secrets?"

I don't mean for my words to turn into a scream or for Rose's teacup to rattle so hard that it flies up and splashes onto her face. Clear droplets land on her otherwise-flawless face, in her curled hair, and all over her crisp white blouse.

Rose's eyes are wide as she looks me up and down. "Calm down this instant, Katrina."

A rush of energy blows through me, like a firehose putting out my anger that sparked from somewhere deep in my chest. I gasp, my anger instantly morphing into familiarity and regret. It's like I'm back in Silver Lake all over again, exposing my emotions through strange events that I'm forced to take the blame for.

"I'm so sorry," I whisper while raising a shaky hand to my mouth.

Will Rose blame me for this? Clearly, she just lost control

of her tea. But even as I try to comfort myself with the explanation, deep down, I know Rose isn't to blame.

I expect her to be upset, to yell, and to kick me out of her home. I don't expect the howling laughter. She's doubled over, unable to contain herself, and tears spring from her eyes.

Charlotte walks in at that moment. Her eyes are wild as she stares between us then assesses Rose's appearance. "What in the heavens?" She hurries over to Rose and attempts to clean her off, but Rose is still laughing. "What happened here?"

I just shake my head, too afraid to speak.

Rose pushes Charlotte's hands away, insisting she's fine. "It was just a little accident," she tells Charlotte before standing and brushing away the wrinkles on her long white skirt. "Come, dear. We'll talk more in my study."

That's all Rose says before she starts to walk. No anger. No resentment. No blame. She's completely nonchalant, as if nothing at all happened. Charlotte gets my attention, breaking me out of my bewildered stare, and gestures for me to hurry and follow Rose. I do, because I can't think of how else to proceed.

Speechless, I follow my grandmother down the hall to her study. Once inside, I take a quick glance around the room and nearly balk at the precious antiques that fill the space. A glittering glass chandelier hangs from the middle of the room, lighting up numerous statues, bookshelves, and glass cases displaying objects that appear too delicate to touch.

Rose sits behind a desk and gestures for me to take a seat on the opposite side.

My eyes catch on the mahogany built-in bookshelf behind Rose. "Are those photo albums?"

She turns to look over her shoulder then reaches for a stack of the books before turning around and dropping them on her desk. A cloud of dust poofs all around it. I wave it away then open the top album and start flipping through the pages. A young couple smiles back at me from the first yellowing black-and-white photograph.

"That's George and me standing on the lot before this home was built. We were so excited to build our dream home here."

"How old were you?"

"I was twenty-eight, your grandfather thirty-two. An older man," she boasts. "Our parents were the best of friends and decided to move here to start the School of Gaia together when we were just kids. I was eighteen when we married, and we immediately started traveling the world. We spent a lot of time in Athens, where we were both born. But after ten years of travel, George and I decided to plant our roots in Apollo Beach to continue what our parents started."

As she's saying that, I flip to a beautiful landscape photo of houses on a hill overlooking the water, followed by other familiar Greek landmarks that I can't name. I can only wish to visit them myself one day.

The next three albums Rose gives me are filled with photos of my mom's teen years. I spend more time flipping through those as Rose tells me about my mom's friends and what she did in her spare time. She was a cheerleader. My mom, a cheer-leader? I never would have believed it, but I can see it for myself. My mom stands in front of the sign for Apollo Beach High School in her long green-and-black skirt and matching sweater.

Halfway through the photo album is when I start to recognize a face appearing in many of the photos, always next to my mother—hugging her, kissing her cheek, holding her hand, studying back-to-back, or chasing her into the water. I realize all too slowly that I'm staring at photos of my father. A pang hits my chest.

"Did your mom tell you how they met?"

My eyes flicker up to see that Rose has been watching me, then I nod. "It's about all she told me." I start to question why she never told me more—and why I never asked. Deep down, I already know the answer. I was afraid to know more, to worsen the feelings of rejection and abandonment that already weighed so heavily on my heart. No one wants to feel unwanted, so I saved myself the pain and rejected the conversation completely.

Rose gives me space for a moment then asks the question that's been lingering in the air. "If you have questions about your father, Katrina, I can answer anything you want to know."

I know she's being sincere, but it's been eighteen years. Of course there is a secret part of me that wondered why he didn't show up after my mom passed away. It's not like he's dead too, but he might as well be. "Where is he?"

Rose frowns. "Now that, unfortunately, is not something I can answer. Not because I don't want to tell you." She's quick to add that last bit. "I just don't know." She searches my eyes as if pleading with me to understand something I can't possibly. "When your mom left, he was never the same. His heart was broken, and he filled his life with distractions I never agreed with. I haven't seen him in quite some time."

I'm tempted to ask about the distractions she's referring to but change my mind quickly. The answer might hurt more than satisfy my hunger for the truth. I flip to the next page in the album and feel overwhelmed. I set the book down and take a few moments to calm myself, dismissing my questions for now.

Rose gestures for me to stand, then I follow her around the room as she shows me the purchases from her trips to Greece. My favorites are easy to pinpoint at first sight. Greek goddess Hera stands with a peacock below her golden skirt, a crown atop her head, and real gold wraps around her body. I remember learning about her in school, and the bronze nameplate on the stand below the marble figure confirms I'm correct.

Inside the glass cases are ancient artifacts, and Rose points out pendants one by one—the Greek owl, cross, horse, sun, and dozens more. All of them have stories, which Rose explains, but I'm barely listening. At this point, I'm too curious about her fascination with Greek culture.

"You have quite the collection. It's like a museum here."

Rose chuckles. "We couldn't help ourselves. The more we traveled, the more we learned, and the more we collected." Rose becomes more animated. "It's amazing how many hidden meanings and stories there are in our history."

"Like what?"

"Look at the meaning of your name, for instance. Katrina

is a variant of the name Katherine, which is derived from the Greek name Aikaterine, which is derived from the Greek name Hecate."

"Hecate, as in the Greek goddess of magic?"

"That's right. Hecate was associated with witchcraft and other forms of the underworld. She was also known as a guardian, the protector of everything newly born. Unfortunately, Hecate's reputation has been greatly misconstrued. If you do the research, you'll discover that the only evil she ever inflicted was to save herself and her family from harm."

"So, what does your name mean?"

"Kind." Rose shrugs. "Not so fancy, I know, but I think it has a nice ring to it." She winks at me. "Come, sit. There is more to discuss."

"What is that?" My eyes are now locked on a glass case in the corner of the room. It sits on a circular platform near the window, rotating at a snail's pace, as the sunlight streams in on it, glinting off the facets of the bulky, odd-shaped crystals inside. If one of those rocks were plucked and shaped, it would look exactly like the necklace from my dream—a radiant pear-shaped gem with a honey-gold casing.

Rose hesitates as my eyes stay glued to the glass case in wonderment. "That is a very rare emerald crystal, dear."

"What makes it so rare?"

She gestures to the stone as if it's obvious. "The size, color, and clarity of it, to begin with. This particular crystal has been in our family for thousands of years. It's a symbol for spiritual awareness, protection, unconditional love, and wisdom. Being gifted with this stone is said to strengthen our connection to the divine energies by opening our hearts and minds. The stone carries healing powers too. Rumor has it that it was a gift from Astina Summer's good friend Aphrodite, the Goddess of Love."

A bubble of laughter escapes my throat. "You say *rumor* like it could actually be real, but you don't actually believe in all this gods stuff."

Rose tilts her head while raising her brows. "Why shouldn't I?"

I scoff, completely baffled by how far Rose is taking all of this ancient Greek mythology madness. "I mean, maybe those people were real, but the stories are obviously embellished."

She raises a brow. "What makes it so unbelievable to you, Katrina?"

I rack my mind, because while it all feels so outrageous to even be discussing, I'm not sure if I ever stopped to ask myself why. "I guess it's all the talk of immortality and light-ning bolts for weapons and driving chariots across the sky."

Rose laughs and places a hand on my shoulder. "Well, I suppose I can see where you're coming from, but you don't need to believe in what I'm telling you right now. We have time."

"Time for what?"

She sweeps her hand around the room. "For all of this to be yours."

Her voice is hushed but filled with a passion that almost makes me feel guilty. "I told you, Rose. I can't stay in Apollo Beach for long." I look at her, hoping she can see the apology that comes from deep within. "I've already made up my mind."

Rose takes in a deep breath then releases it slowly. "But you'll stay at least until your birthday, yes?"

I blink, once again feeling like I'm missing something. "Of course."

Rose smiles, a satisfied twinkle in her eyes. "Well, then I guess I have a couple of weeks to change your mind."

TWELVE

ose, Charlotte, and I are eating dinner the next night when someone knocks on the front door. Rose perks up like she's expecting someone, but then she turns to me. "Do you mind getting that, dear?"

The way Rose's eyes light up with a hint of a smirk makes me suspicious. "Um, okay." I dart a look between her and Charlotte before setting my napkin on the table and leaving the room.

I don't know why my nerves are all aflutter as I walk from the dining room, through the great room, and into the foyer. By the time I place my hand on the knob to pull open the door, my heart is working triple-time. When the door opens and I see who's standing outside, I can't believe my eyes.

"Alec? What are you doing here?"

He grins, and my knees weaken. He looks ridiculously gorgeous in a white shirt and dark jeans that are ripped at one knee. His thick hair is styled back with a classic side part that lifts high off his head. If Rose hadn't gifted me the pretty pink off-the-shoulder dress I'm wearing now, then I would probably feel underdressed.

"I was heading to Island Grille to meet up with some friends and thought maybe you'd want to come with. I know I invited you to my Fourth of July party, but that's still a few weeks out. It's time to make some friends, Summer Girl." He winks, causing my stomach to flip.

Summer Girl. No one has ever called me that before, but I guarantee I wouldn't have found it half as flattering coming from anyone else. "I don't know if I should." Although my heart is screaming to say yes, my insecurities outweigh it. "Your friends don't exactly like me. Your girlfriend, Iris, especially."

He pinches his brows together. "Iris isn't my girlfriend, and neither of them know you. The rest of my friends haven't met you."

His words are few and simple, but I can see the sincerity behind his eyes and hear the honesty in his tone. Alec Stone is a rare gem who just might change things for me if I give him a chance. He knows how his friends feel about me, yet he wants me to hang out anyway.

"True," I say slowly, a smile creeping onto my face.

"You're not going to make me beg, are you? Because you should know, I'm not above begging. In fact, I'm one of those guys who loves the chase. The more you turn me down, the more effort I'll put in. And that's the honest truth."

I laugh, a real laugh that comes straight from my gut. It's been a long time since I've done that. "Okay, fine." I hold up my hand. "But you better not be setting me up for some kind of prank or new girl initiation or something."

"I promise, no pranks, and the only initiation you might have to suffer through is a game of pool with me. I'm pretty good. The humiliation you might face from losing will set the tone for the rest of your life in this town." He shrugs, a sparkle in his eyes. "No big deal."

I bite down on my lip and step back from the entrance. "I'll need to let Rose know."

Not even a second passes. "It's fine with me, dear. I heard." Rose shouts her permission from the dining room. "Have a good time."

My heart races when I realize Rose was listening the entire time. I roll my eyes while Alec laughs, then I step back across the threshold. "I guess that means I'm all yours."

The way Alec looks at me next—with a lingering stare while his smile slips from his lips and desire lights up his eyes—it does dangerous things to my core. "Lucky me."

He shoves his hands in his pockets, gives me a sideways grin, then leads me to his lifted white truck. It's not until I'm strapped inside that I take my first deep breath since seeing Alec standing at my front door. This feels a lot like a date, but I know it would be crazy for me to even entertain the thought of Alec wanting more than friendship with me. He's gorgeous, and I'm...

Alec opens his driver's-side door before I can finish my own negative thought, then we're rolling toward the gates of Summer Island with the windows down and the wind blowing through our hair. He blasts a rock song I'm vaguely familiar with, and I'm almost relieved the music is too loud for us to carry on a conversation. I'm still reeling from the fact that he showed up at my door, so I take the ride to Summer Island to steady my nerves.

It seems to work, until we park and I see just how packed

the restaurant is. Lights dance from the inside stage, where a band is jamming out. Loud voices and laughter carry into the parking lot, and smoke rises from the chimney over the kitchen. It seems like the entire town is here.

"So, this is a crazy night out in Apollo Beach, huh?" I ask Alec after we meet at the front of his truck.

He leans against one of his headlights, indicating he's in no rush to go inside. "This is it. Not such a boring old town, is it?"

I shake my head and stand beside him so we're looking at the restaurant. "I definitely don't think it's a boring old town. The opposite, actually. I think it's beautiful here. And I'm not just talking about the beach. This island alone is—" I struggle to find the right word. Unique. Mystical. Picturesque. Nothing quite fits how I feel.

"A little slice of heaven?" He peers sideways at me with hopeful eyes.

"Okay, sure. Let's go with that. I still can't get over that my family created all of this. I had no idea."

Confusion spreads across his face. "Really? You didn't know about the island or your family's role in the development of this town?"

I shrug, knowing this is a big admission to someone I barely know. Something tells me I can trust Alec, though. "All of it. My mom never spoke with my grandparents. I never met my grandma, except for just after I was born. It's like I woke up one morning and was transported into a whole new world."

Sadness flickers in his eyes and guilt rushes through me. The last thing I want is Alec's pity. "What about your dad?"

"He was never part of my life."

Alec shakes his head. "Geez. I'm sorry, Kat."

I push away from his truck, not wanting to continue down this dark, depressing road. "Don't be. He's the one missing out, right?"

Alec gives a firm nod. "Absolutely." His gaze slips from my face, to my dress, and back up. "You're a tough chick, aren't you?"

His question makes me laugh. No one has ever called me that before. "Depends how you look at it, I guess."

He tilts his head. "What does that mean?"

I bite down on my lip, not sure how much I should tell him about my past. He's clearly curious about me, even though I'm not sure why. But I don't want that curiosity to turn into something else. Like fear or disappointment. There's a twisting in my gut. "Not all things are what they appear to be, Alec. You may see a tough chick, but maybe that's because I don't want you to see the truth."

"And what's your truth, Kat Summer?"

Air pushes up my throat, resembling a laugh. "That I'm completely and utterly lost."

The corners of his mouth tips up into a smile. "Aren't we all?"

A gust of wind blows, wrapping me in his crisp, cool scent. He even smells perfect. I could salivate over this guy. From head to toe, he's a dream. "I think you're a charmer, Alec Stone." The smile that reaches his eyes tells me he knows it's true.

"Only when I want to be." He winks again, causing my

insides to heat, then he wraps his hand around mine and squeezes. "What do you say? Think we've stalled enough?"

My eyes go straight to where our hands connect, and I wonder what his friends will think when they see us like this. He must sense my nervousness because he gives a gentle squeeze. "Or we can stay here and talk."

A loud crunch of gravel jerks my attention back to the parking lot, where a figure is crossing near us. *Crunch, crunch, crunch.* The man doesn't look in our direction, but I know it's Johnny. I get the odd sense that he's already spotted us. Maybe it's the tension in his broad back or the hard lock he holds on his jaw beneath the faint scruff. Or maybe it's the way he's walking so close to Alec's truck rather than on the dirt pathway that leads directly to the restaurant, where he should be about to start his shift.

I swallow and watch him gain distance.

"Kat? What do you want to do?"

"Um." I'm jostled back to my conversation with Alec, and I quickly try to remember the question. "We can go in. I need to know if you're really as good at pool as you say you are."

He grins like he's accepting a challenge, then we start walking. A group of Alec's friends are already standing around one of the pool tables. I recognize some of them from the beach volleyball game. Iris and Ava are there, their eyes on us—specifically on where Alec's hand is releasing mine.

"Kat, hey!" Trisha's arms are around my neck before I've even looked at her. "I'm so glad you're here. What did you decide? Are you coming in on Monday or what?"

I open my mouth to respond then catch Johnny stepping

behind the bar, tossing a towel over his shoulder. *Does he ever smile?* Annoyance shakes through me. "I haven't decided yet," I finally tell her.

The corners of her mouth push down in a dramatic pout. "Anything I can do to change your mind?"

I laugh. "I need to give it to everyone in this town. You all are a persistent bunch."

Before Trisha can respond, Alec tugs me away and introduces me to Brett, along with a bunch of others whose names I know I won't remember tomorrow.

"We're about to play a game," Brett says with an uptick of his head. "You two want in? We need a fourth." He's standing beside Iris when he says it.

"Yeah, we'll play. Right, Kat? This can be practice for when we play each other later."

He winks, and I make a cringe face at Alec, suddenly feeling put on the spot. "I've never played pool before."

Iris rolls her eyes. "Perfect." She leans her pool stick toward Alec. "You brought her here. She's on your team."

That fiery sensation that never leads to anything good is already building deep in my chest.

"Sounds like a good plan," Alec answers easily, then he's pulling me to the wall to help me find my own stick. "Don't worry. I'll teach you everything you need to know. We'll beat 'em." He chuckles, cooling the sparks that came alive moments ago.

When we walk back over to the table, Brent is racking the balls in a triangular shape while Iris and Ava huddle together, looking annoyed. The whole mean-girl act is already getting old, so I have no problem ignoring it for as long as I have to.

Alec insists I go first. He helps me position the cue in my hands. His body is close to mine. His warm breath floats over my shoulder, creating a wave of goosebumps on my skin. Once I have the positioning right, he takes a step back. "Now pull back a little and then tap the white ball so that it hits that solid blue ball. That's your best shot."

I do as he says, pulling back the stick then pushing it forward to hit the white ball. The white ball flies toward the blue one and smacks it dead in the center. I must have pushed too hard, though, because the blue ball leaps off the table, soars across the room, and lands somewhere on the floor.

Humiliated, I clutch my hot cheek with one hand and look toward Alec. He's doubled over in a fit of laughter, and he's not the only one. I don't know whether to join them or cry from embarrassment.

"What an idiot," Ava mutters to Iris.

Meanwhile, Trisha is cheering me on, and Alec is jogging across the room in search of the ball. When he comes back, he's still laughing. He wraps his arms around me in a giant hug and squeezes. "Now, let's just work on your control."

I don't have to see myself in the mirror to know my face is beet red with a blush. But we continue the game, watching as Iris and Brett pull ahead a few balls, leaving it up to Alec to save our game. Then it's my turn again.

"Okay, Kat. You're up. Keep the ball on the table this time." Alec flashes a smile at me, and the heat rises in my face.

I eye the table, planning my next move, and notice a solid ball near the middle pocket. To get to it, I'll have to somehow get the white ball around from behind a striped one. If I hit its side, it could bounce off it and hit the yellow solid right into the pocket. I position myself, eyes focused, figuring I have nothing to lose.

"Whoa, getting fancy," Alec says when he sees what I'm about to do.

"Oh great," Ava says dryly. "Everybody duck."

As I pull back on the stick, I look directly at Ava and glare. My eyes aren't even back on the ball when I push the stick forward, this time with much less force. The tip of my cue hits the white ball perfectly, pushing the white ball to the side wall so it moves around the striped ball, smacks directly into the yellow one, and sends the yellow ball into the pocket.

Alec cheers loudly from the opposite end of the table while Brett stands there with his mouth wide open. Iris and Ava stand off to the side, wearing incredulous expressions. I'm so shocked and elated, I yank the pool stick back from the table, not paying attention to what's behind me. When the stick connects with something hard and all momentum stops, a shooting pain fires from my hands to my forearms. Horrified, I turn to see what I struck.

Johnny stands there, leaning over slightly, his red-faced expression filled with pain, and he's clutching his stomach. I jolt toward him and place my hand on his shoulder without thinking. His arm stiffens before he shakes me off, but not before I can feel the strength beneath the fabric.

"I'm so sorry. I was excited, and I wasn't paying attention."

"You're trouble." He growls the words so low that only I can hear, and I hear his warning loud and clear. "Do yourself a favor and stay the hell away from me."

With a glare, he leaves me completely shaken to the core.

THIRTEEN

A s soon as my feet hit the sand the next morning, I feel free. I take off on a jog along the shore, breathing in the salty air from the bay as my legs ease into their natural cadence. After my mother's death, I was in no mood to exercise, but after weeks of feeling like I've been locked in one place, my energy is practically bursting to break free.

I'm surprised by how quickly I find my rhythm. It's like riding a bike, and it's all coming back to me. At times, I feel like I can jog for hours. I get lost in my thoughts and let my feet take me where they lead. This feels like one of those times. Still, I try to pace my steps so I don't overexert myself.

I continue past the neighboring homes until I reach the public beach just outside of Summer Estate. To the left, I stare down a strip of rock that juts into the bay and instinctively move toward it. I climb over the jagged rocks, one by one, taking cautious steps as water slaps over the rocks on either side of me. Once I'm at the end of the rock pier, I take a seat on one of the taller rocks and let my feet dangle over it. Water crashes the rocks around me, a melody fitting to such a turbulent past few weeks. This is the first time in a while I've felt anything close to peaceful. I can breathe.

"There you are." Alec sits beside me, a smile on his handsome face and a twinkle of curiosity in his eyes. "Living on the edge, I see."

I let out a light laugh and look back out over the water. "Hardly. I was going for a run and got distracted by this—" I search for a word unsuccessfully. "Anyway, why does everything in this town seem so different?"

Alec shrugs. "Ask your grandmother. But my guess is that a lot of heart went into developing this town. Everywhere you turn, there's a piece of history embedded in what you see."

I frown. "It sounds like my grandparents have done a lot for this town. I mean, Rose clearly loves it here."

Alec cocks his head to the side. "Why wouldn't she?"

Heat rises in my cheeks. "I just mean that I don't understand why there are people in this town who don't approve of the work Rose is doing. Bettering the environment, enriching the businesses and services already local to this place, and minimizing the overcrowding that comes with tourism. I feel like I'm missing something."

Alec stares at me for a long time before finally speaking. "I don't think it's you who's missing something, Kat. Some people in this town are..." He releases a smile as he looks down at the rock and runs his finger along a small crack in its surface. "Greedy, neglectful, selfish. I could go on."

He lifts his brows at me, and I smile. "Rose says the same thing."

"So, Summer Girl, what do you plan on doing this

summer, besides contemplating the fortress your family built?"

I don't miss the abrupt change in conversation, but part of me is grateful for it.

"School," I say. "Virtual school, to be exact. I still have a few classes to finish up so I can graduate. Rose insists I get it over with."

"Ah, that's a bummer if that's how you're going to spend your first summer here. You'll have to find some time to get away and hang out with us."

I nod then look back at Alec, realizing I have no idea how old he is. "What about you?"

"I just graduated. I'll be starting at the private college in the fall."

"The School of Gaia?"

Alec nods. "The one and only. You'll be going there in the fall, right? I figured with you being a Summer and all..."

When I was bored last night, I looked up the School of Gaia just to see what it's all about. From what I read, its focus is on environmental science, engineering, and medicine, but there are arts programs as well. While it's all fascinating, I haven't put much thought into what I would study in college. I don't think I would have ever considered something like oceanography, atmospheric chemistry, or any of the topics of study found on the long list I looked over.

"I don't think I'll be attending. I might not even be in Apollo Beach for much longer."

I hate how my heart grows heavy when I see the disappointment on Alec's face.

"What? Really?"

I shrug as a strange feeling of guilt snakes through me. I'm not sure why. It's not like I have any sort of connection to this town, but even as I think that, I know it's not totally true. "I don't know. If I left, I don't even know where I would go."

"Stay." It's a simple word, but the force behind it hits me straight in the gut. I look up to see Alec's gaze grip hold of mine. "You have to stay."

I want to ask him why, but deep down, I already know, so I suck in a deep breath instead. "I should get back to my run."

He helps me stand, and I can't help but stare at his dimpled smile one more time. "Can I join? I need to see if you're as good at running as you are at pool."

I laugh. "Okay, fine. Just do your best to keep up."

He chuckles, and we take the rocky pathway carefully before landing back on the beach. I let Alec set our pace—a light jog farther along the coastline.

I'm fully aware of the fact that he seems to be holding back. "You can go faster, you know? I can handle it."

He meets my gaze with a challenge then nods before taking off with more force. We zoom in and out of the small neighborhoods around the own. It's as if our path is tracing out the shape of a star. When we're turning around at the marina, I realize just how amazing I feel. My legs feel stronger than ever. Every muscle, large and small, expands and contracts with each motion. The deep breaths I'm able to pull in as I run is as impressive as my need to go faster.

The only thing that slows me down is the view of the seemingly abandoned area of town as we approach it. It's as if Apollo Beach is split into two—north and south, new and old. Even the sand in the volleyball area appears to be abandoned as weeds grow between its grains in the shallow spots. All that's left are crumbling exteriors and overgrown lawns the color of dried mustard. A strange feeling takes hold in my chest, like there's a history here I'll never understand.

When we get close to the start of a wooden walkway with a sign that points to a "Nature Trail," I slow alongside him and look over for the first time since we started our run. He's sweating and breathing heavily. I assume I should be just as tired, but my energy isn't exhausted.

"You've got to be kidding me," he says while sucking in sips of air. "How do you have so much energy?"

I twist my lips into a hesitant smile. "I don't know, honestly. I haven't run in weeks. It must be all that built-up energy from staying in so much lately."

Alec shakes his head. "That would make it harder, not easier. We just ran five miles, and you haven't even broken a sweat. You are a superhuman, woman."

I laugh at his strange compliment then step forward onto a concrete path that eventually turns to dirt and rocks. We walk the rest of the way, and tropical wildlife begins to spring from the ground on either side of us. As the walkway narrows, exotic leaves and flowers on either side brush my arms.

Alec is apparently a wealth of knowledge. He describes what I'm seeing around me—tidal creeks where the mangroves grow, providing a habitat for large coastal birds, oysters, crabs, and fish. We move up a small hill, round a corner, then travel back down to an empty semi-enclosed beachfront. I look up to find a large building with the same smokestacks I remember seeing upon my arrival to Apollo Beach.

When we finally reach a clearing at the top of the trail, I get a better view of the energy plant as it looms before me. Tall cylinder structures attached to a rectangular building overlook the water, with a fenced-in yard of gravel surrounding all sides of the facility.

My mom once mentioned that my father worked at an energy plant after high school. This must be the one. The thought creates a heaviness in my chest—an unwelcome weight that I've always tried to avoid. Being here, at the birthplace of my father, the place where my parents fell in love, it feels impossible to escape.

Sadness tries to dominate my memories of her, but this time, I won't allow it. I'll never stop missing my mother, but I refuse to cry every time I think of her. Instead, I focus on the good times we shared. A smile plays across my face as I immerse myself in a nostalgic place where time no longer exists.

Time passes, but I remain still as memories of my mom flash through my mind like a moving picture book. Her bright smile as I came through the door after playing basketball. Her quick-paced walk everywhere she went, always in a hurry. Our bicycle races. The warm hugs she gave me when I occasionally revealed my insecurities to her. The silly faces she would make when I asked her about a date. No one was good enough for her. I'll never forget the sight of her reading the newspaper every morning as she sat on the couch, holding a fresh cup of coffee. Her scent after her nightly shower was always fresh from the baby powder she sprinkled all over her body.

By the time we step back onto the private beach in front of our homes, I'm exhausted. Not physically, though. I could run another ten miles. Mentally, I'm just done.

It's like Alec reads my mind. "Come on."

He pulls me toward the shore and kicks off his shoes, then he slides off his shirt and tosses it onto the sand. I quickly avert my gaze but not before catching sight of a well-sculpted chest and abs. *Geez, he's got a good body.* I saw him shirtless that first night on the beach, but this is somehow different. We're alone now, and daylight leaves nothing to the imagination.

I hesitate for a second before following his lead, stripping out of my tank top and shoes, leaving my sports bra and my shorts on. He grins then grips my hand again before pulling me to the water.

We both take a running dive and come up when only our faces and necks clear the water. We're both laughing as our eyes connect, and I swear there's a crackling and sizzling from our connection like there are electrically charged particles lighting up the air. And in that strange but electrifying moment, I imagine he might kiss me. I want him to kiss me. I want it so badly that I almost miss the way he's wrapping his arms around my waist and pulling me closer.

A shiver races through my body, and even while my nerves are lighting off like fireworks, I'm shocked by how comfortable I am in his hold. It's all so natural with Alec. So easy. So right. I don't even flinch when he brings his face closer to mine, and my lips start to tingle in anticipation of his kiss.

My first kiss.

My thoughts are racing. Fear of the unknown wreaks havoc, causing my heart to gallop so loud in my chest I'm certain Alec can hear it. Then his mouth presses to mine, tasting of saltwater, while his hold around my waist tightens. I move my lips back against his, testing the way they feel matched with mine, familiarizing myself with their shape, their taste, and their firmness. We've only started to find our rhythm when the moment is ruined with a few sprinkles, followed by a heavy downpour of rain.

A hungry rumble tears through the sky, startling us and causing us to jump slightly, enough to separate us. A bolt of lightning follows with a deafening crack.

As if reading each other's mind, we take off for the shore and stumble away from the water. Alec runs ahead and scrambles to grab our things, then we trip along the shore's edge toward our homes.

"Thanks for the run!" I shout. The wind whips my hair around my head, smacking me hard in the face.

He squeezes my hand like he never wants to let go. "Want to do it again tomorrow?"

My hesitation has nothing to do with how much I like Alec. Liking him is the easy part. It's the leaving him part that I'm starting to fear. "I don't know if that's such a good idea."

He frowns. "Why not? We have fun together, don't we? And your grandmother loves me."

I laugh as an uneasy feeling whips through me. "My grandmother loves you? How would you even know that?"

Something flickers in his eyes, and the playful smile falls from his face, triggering a warning in my gut. "I mean... I-I think she does. She was quick to let you come out with me last night, wasn't she?"

Something feels wrong. He's lying. My intuition is strong on this one. Tiny puzzle pieces begin to click together in my brain. How insistent Rose was that I stay in Apollo Beach. How she seemed to already know who was at the door when Alec picked me up last night.

My jaw drops as it all hits me like a barrel being dropped on my dreams. I should have known it was all a lie. "Rose asked you to invite me out last night." My voice is shaking, I'm so angry.

Alec's face completely crumbles, illuminating his truth brighter than the lightning that strikes the water behind him. "Yes, but—"

I shake my head and take a step back. My entire body is trembling now. "I don't know what she told you, but I don't need a pity friendship. Whatever she offered you in return, I hope it was worth it."

He's frowning, his forehead deeply creased in the center. "Kat, just listen for a minute. It's not like—"

He starts to move toward me, but I'm gaining distance more quickly than he can close it.

"Leave me alone, Alec. I'm warning you. You don't want to be near me right now."

As if the sky is listening, a loud rumble shakes overhead. Alec jumps and looks toward the noise. I use the distraction as an opportunity to flee back to Summer Manor... and to leave Alec Stone behind.

FOURTEEN

The main doors to Island Grille are locked when I arrive Monday morning, so I meander around the porch to check out the view while I wait. I lean forward onto the balcony rail and look out at the open sea. The sun is rising above the horizon, creating a mirror image on the calm water as birds soar through the sky. I'm in a terrible mood thanks to how last night ended with Alec, which was followed by a confrontation with Rose. Despite that, it's a beautiful day, and I intend to enjoy it.

"What are you doing?"

I jump and spin around to glare at the intruder to my thoughts. It's Johnny. A very disheveled, tousled hair, and tired-eyed version of him. My heart quickens in my chest, and I don't know if it's from my eyeful of the guy or the way he snuck up on me just now.

"Geez. You don't have to yell at me."

He twists his lips like he's looking at a weirdo. "I didn't yell." Then he turns and starts to walk back around the corner. "Come on. I need to count the till. *You* need to fold napkins."

My eyes are glued to his black shirt as it ripples over a plethora of muscles beneath it. "Fun," I say under my breath so he doesn't hear me.

At least, I hoped he wouldn't. But the way his steps slow for a half of a second make me realize I should be more careful. While he's nice to look at, he's not exactly the most pleasant person to be around. Working an entire shift with him will surely be torture.

He walks me into the bar and over to a booth where a basket of blue cloth napkins sit. "You can fold these and wrap the silverware inside like this." He takes a fork, a knife, and a spoon, places them in a folded napkin and rolls the napkin until everything is snug.

I shouldn't be mesmerized by the fluidity of Johnny's napkin-folding skills. Nor should I be comparing the size of his thick, calloused hands to Alec's soft ones. He's too much of a hot-headed jerk for me to notice those kinds of things.

"I hope you were taking notes." He points at the basket and walks away. "Get to work."

A burning sensation runs through my veins as I watch him strut away. At least he hasn't glared at me yet. Maybe things are looking up.

I start wrapping the silverware the way he showed me. It's a monotonous, boring job, but I guess someone has to do it. I glance up to see Johnny standing at the cash register, facing the other direction, and frown. I would love to know what I did to deserve his cold shoulder. It seemed all I had to do was move to town. I could ask him, but then he would get the satisfaction of my curiosity.

After wrapping another napkin, I get a better idea. Who

wants a boring rolled-up napkin when they can have some-thing more creative—like the shape of a sun? I jump into a rhythm that sends my hands flying into repetitive motion. I'm done in minutes. When I stand and look up with a satis-fied grin, Johnny is standing there with a strange look on his face.

"That was fast."

I look at my handiwork and shrug. "It was easy. What's next?"

The top of my head only reaches his collarbone, so I have to lift my chin to meet his gaze. He stares down with a heated intensity that could fry an egg. From here, I get a good look at the scar that runs from the side of his eye to the top of his right cheek. It takes everything in me to contain my shudder as I imagine him in some sort of biker brawl that he most likely won.

His eyes flicker down to the table—to my masterpiece. He lifts one of the cloth suns, shakes out the silverware, and dangles it in front of him. "What the hell is this?"

My words are lost at first. I swallow my nerves and stand up straighter. "Anyone can roll a napkin. These"—I give an excited wave of my hand—"are fun."

"I don't remember asking for *fun*." With a shake of his wrist, the napkin unravels, and he tosses it on the table. "Fix them all."

I drop into my seat, mouth agape. Johnny walks toward the kitchen, and I am utterly speechless. I know he's rude, but I'm not sure if his growl is worse than his bite. Frustra-tion consumes me, and as soon as he's out of sight, I'm making quick work of the task he gave me, undoing what I created and rewrapping the silverware the way he instructed.

Not enough time has passed, and I'm still fuming when I lift myself from the seat and march into the staff room to confront Johnny. He has no right to talk to me like that.

I slam the door open with my palm, ready to let him have it, when I get an eyeful of his shirtless form sliding a shirt over his head. He's facing me, his face covered by his shirt's fabric, so he doesn't see the way I ogle the deep carvings that define his abs and the scar that starts near one side of the V that dips into his shorts and reaches around his back. I should turn away or run—anything else but stand here and stare.

His shirt slides over his eyes, and he's staring back at me.

My cheeks warm and my breathing is unsteady. "I-I'm sorry."

He says nothing about my gawking. Instead, he grabs a black shirt on the counter beside him and chucks it at me. When I open the balled-up material, I notice it's a work tank top with Island Grille's logo on it.

"Thank you." The words are barely a whisper as they leave my mouth.

Johnny slides past me and walks out the door, allowing me to change in private.

For the millionth time, I debate whether a job here is worth it. I don't want to quit before I've even been hired, and I don't want to let a grumpy asshole like Johnny get the better of me, but I don't know how I can work with the guy long-term.

After changing into the work tank, I find an empty locker

to toss my shirt into. When I walk out of the staff room, Johnny is leaning against the opposite wall, arms folded across his chest.

He tosses me a stained white cloth that smells of cleaning solution. "You can wipe down the tables and set the chairs out."

I narrow my eyes and fold my arms to mirror him. "Oh yeah? And what are you going to do?"

He raises his brows, as if accepting my challenge. "Clean the bathrooms. Why? Wanna swap?"

I let my arms fall, feeling deflated. It's if he won some sort of battle, and I'm too annoyed to answer.

He rolls his eyes and pushes off the wall. "Didn't think so."

After heading back out to the restaurant, I spend the next thirty minutes wiping down each table and placing the chairs in their respective positions. It's enough time for me to get my head straight again and remember that Johnny is harmless compared to Steve. Sure, Johnny hates me for some mysterious reason, but he isn't doing anything more than being rude. I can deal with rude.

Once he's done with the bathrooms, he shows me how to take an order and place it into the system then how to charge a customer's card to close out a table. Meanwhile, I just listen and take it all in, doing everything in my power to avoid eye contact and speaking to him. If I open my mouth to say anything, I know it won't be nice.

"Monday mornings are never busy, so it's just you and me for the first hour. I'll shadow you and tell you everything you need to fix."

My eyes widen, and I see there's a twinkle in his eyes to tell me he's actually joking. Not that he's being playful. He's just enjoying being an ass. "Oh gee, what a great guy you are."

"Yeah, well, I wouldn't go that far. Just looking forward to watching you fail."

Fire flares in my chest, and I'm not willing to back down this time. "Excuse me? What is your problem? You've been nasty to me since you laid eyes on me. I'm sorry I hit you when I was playing pool the other day. It was an accident, but you were terrible to me before that. So what gives?"

Johnny starts to open his mouth, but the door swings open.

Roy walks in. "Hey, Kat," he greets with a big smile. "Don't mess up." He salutes, then he walks straight to the back, most likely to his office.

When I look back at Johnny, I swear there's a tiny smirk lifting his cheeks. When I let out a little growl and open my mouth to prompt him to answer my question, Johnny places his hands on my shoulders and swivels me toward the door. "Your first customer. Let's see what you've got."

For the next hour, I take all the distractions I can get. Customers enter, and I rush to seat them. I get their drinks then take their orders. At some point, Johnny gets busy at the bar, and I no longer feel like I'm putting on a show for him. After other staff members and customers arrive, I feel like I'm thriving in the chaos of tending to multiple orders at once.

When I pick up an order from the kitchen, I find Johnny and Roy near the break room, standing close together and speaking about something. I find it interesting to watch Johnny interact with someone without the grumpy face he always seems to wear around me.

Roy sees me standing in the kitchen and waves. "Hey, Kat. You're doing good out there."

I smile at the old man, happy to have pleased someone.

"Order up!" Mikey calls, snapping my attention toward him. He winks, and I grab the sizzling breakfast skillets off the warmers.

"Whoa!" Johnny calls out before running over to me and blocking my way to the dining area. He looks down at what I'm holding, his expression twisting in confusion. "Those skillets aren't too hot for your hands? Most people use the oven pads to grab them."

I shrug. "My hands are tough, I guess."

He shakes his head as if he doubts me. Meanwhile, my heart is fluttering wildly, partially because of our proximity and partially because I know that I might smack him if he says another rude thing to me.

"You're doing good," he says with a frown. "Beginners luck, I guess."

I look up, daring myself, and catch a partial smile from Johnny. My flutters catch in my throat. If he weren't such a jerk, he would be extremely attractive.

A jolt of excitement swells my chest. "Does that mean I'm hired?"

Johnny looks over his shoulder toward where he was standing with Roy, but Roy is gone. "I don't know. We'll call you if you are. You can go."

I stare back at him, mystified. I don't know why, but

something feels so off with what he's telling me. "But you just told me I did good."

He grabs the skillets from my hands and stares me dead in the eyes. "I also just told you that you can go."

With that, he backs out through the swinging doors and walks straight toward my table.

FIFTEEN

Today marks the start of the eighteenth year of my life, a milestone that Rose believes to be cause for a celebration. I, on the other hand, have been dreading everything about it and am currently contemplating an escape. It's either that, or I'll be forced to walk down those spiral steps and make nice with dozens of strangers.

My stomach knots as I stare out the open doors of my balcony while the sun makes its ascent against a bright-blue backdrop. It's only ten in the morning, and the party is already in full swing downstairs. I can hear the guests' happy chatter, smell the hot catering dishes, and feel every ounce of excitement reverberating through every inch of the house.

The door to my room opens a crack, and Charlotte pokes her head through, a sympathetic look on her face. "It's time, Kat. Are you ready?"

I let out a nervous laugh and shake my head. "Definitely not."

Charlotte frowns. "What's wrong? Besides your tiff with Rose."

I chew my bottom lip while my anxiety eats away at me. I'm still upset at Rose for going behind my back to get Alec to take me out, but that's not what's bothering me today. "I think Rose's wild stories and crazy imaginings are getting the better of me."

She steps into my room and shuts the door. "Why do you say that?"

I swallow. "I had another dream last night."

Charlotte looks to be considering her words. Then she waves me over to the vanity desk to sit. "Come. Tell me all about it while I do your hair and makeup."

I shake my head. "I don't want makeup."

She sighs. "Must you always be so stubborn? Come. Sit."

The sternness in her tone causes my heart to jump, and I do as she says. While she lightly applies foundation to my face, I tell her all about my first dream and why this one haunts me more. "My dream last night was the same—except the girl in the mirror wasn't me this time. It was Rose."

I shudder at the memory of waking up in a cold sweat. I didn't plan to tell Charlotte, but I also didn't expect the dream to weigh so heavily on my heart, like I'm supposed to be decoding something important.

"Perhaps your dream was a combination of things. You've been pretty upset at your grandmother. I would aim to guess that your anger toward Rose, combined with your nerves about today, could certainly stir up your imagination."

I bow my head. "I suppose. But do you blame me? What Rose did was so embarrassing."

Charlotte is silent for a beat. "Rose is a woman who gets

what she wants. In this case, she wants you to stay in Apollo Beach. Her methods were—"

"Wrong," I cut in before Charlotte can make an excuse for her.

She sighs. "Yes, but Alec didn't have to agree. It's not like Rose paid him off or anything."

I frown. "How do I know that?"

Rose insists all she did was ask Alec to befriend me. But for some reason, that still doesn't sit right with me.

"Because," Charlotte says, "Rose is a very powerful woman in the position she's in because of her honesty. She has no reason to lie to you, Kat." She gives me a reassuring smile and backs away. "All done. Do you want me to walk with you?"

I shake my head and watch as she steps back out of my room and softly closes the door behind her. It doesn't matter how deeply hurt I still am. Unfortunately, in Rose's eyes, that betrayal doesn't release me from my duties as a Summer. That's what she called my presence at my own birthday party. A duty.

Filling my lungs with the deepest breath I can take, I pause in front of the vanity mirror to take one final glance at myself. I have to admit, the green baby-doll chiffon dress Charlotte picked for me is gorgeous. It's strapless with a heart-shaped bodice, and it flows down to a couple of inches above my knees. Simple touches like mascara and blush accentuate my long eyelashes and rosy cheeks. Light eyeliner defines my light-blue eyes, which seem to be becoming a brighter gray with every day that passes. But it's my hair that strikes me the most. The length alone has grown so much over the few short weeks, from the tips of my shoulders to halfway down my back. Seeing my reflection now, I'm thankful Charlotte insisted on curling it.

When I reach the top of the spiral staircase, I peer over the rail and down into the great room. It's as if I'm over-looking a scene from a Mardi Gras parade, with explosions of color decorating the room. Generous arrangements of food and beverages are lined up on a long table, a folk band plays spirited music from the corner, and arrangements of white flowers are sprinkled just about everywhere. The cele-bration looks more like a summer solstice celebration than a birthday party, and for that, I'm grateful.

My heart takes off at a canter as I take my first tottering steps down the staircase. I've never worn heels before, and it was probably a mistake to start today. Strangers stare up at me from the foyer, their smiles making me look away as they welcome me to my own party. A queasiness churns my stomach the closer I get to the circus below. I'm so focused on the forced smile on my face that I completely miss a stair and lose my balance on the final step.

An arm shoots out and wraps my waist, steadying me before I can topple onto the marble floor. I'm staring down at the strong arm wrapped in black fabric that buttons at the wrist and my heart jumps into my throat. *It can't be.* I snap my head up to find myself staring directly into the devas-tating blue eyes of Johnny Pierce.

"What are you doing here?"

He might have just saved me from major embarrass-ment, but his glare is no different than when I saw him last. Then his brows rise, and he glances over at his other arm currently holding a tray of appetizers. "What does it look like to you?"

I roll my eyes and step away from him, patting down my dress like my near spill was powerful enough to wrinkle it. "Of course," I mutter sarcastically under my breath. "I didn't know Island Grille catered."

Johnny averts his gaze, but not before I see him check out my dress. "For someone who wanted a job, you sure failed to do your research."

My mouth drops open. The audacity of this man is inconceivable. "Well, lucky for you, I don't want the job anymore, so research isn't necessary."

"Good to know. I'll let Roy know."

"What are you talking about? It's been two weeks. You said you'd call if I got the job."

He shrugs. "Haven't gotten around to it yet." Then he swings his tray in front of me, so I get an eyeful of the spread of toast and diced tomato. "Care for some bruschetta?"

I wrinkle my nose and shake my head. "I'll pass. Thank you."

When I turn away, Rose is walking through the foyer toward me. "There you are. Katrina, you look stunning." She gives me a long once-over then places a quick kiss on my cheek. "Happy birthday, dear." She leans in and whispers into my ear, "I know you're still upset with me, but today is a very important day. I hope you'll put aside your frustration and enjoy it. Will you?" She looks so hopeful waiting for my response.

After a moment of stubborn pause, I nod.

She smiles back brightly. "Oh, good. Now that we've

gotten that out of the way. I have something for you." She holds up a headpiece made from branches and white wild-flowers then places it on my head without asking permission. She leans back, admiring my appearance. "Perfect."

Rose ushers me into the great room, where the majority of the crowd is gathered. As she does, I can't help noticing how vibrant she looks in her white short-sleeved dress with a sash made from the same cloth draped diagonally across one shoulder and down to her hip.

"Oh, dear," Rose says, her eyes on something over on the other side of the room. "I'll be right back. Mingle, eat, have fun." Her eyes twinkle before she walks away, and I'm left standing by myself at my own party, among a group of people I know nothing about. Awkward.

A gray-haired woman in a long white gown with a brown belt and wearing a grandiose smile is the first to approach. "You must be the birthday girl. Rose has told us so much about you." She places her hands on my shoulders, pulling me forward slightly to touch my cheek with her lips. My body jerks toward her. "I'm Darla French, and this is my husband, Darryl."

I peek over her shoulder to find a man with glittery gold face paint around his eyes.

Peeling myself away from the strong woman, I smile at them. "It's nice to meet you both."

Darryl takes my hand, raising it to his mouth to plant a light kiss on the back. "Welcome to Apollo Beach. I'm sorry we haven't had a chance to come by to see you before now."

I'm not sure how to respond to that, so I go with something different. "How do you know my grandmother?"

Cursed

"We work together at Enchantment Theater on Summer Island." She's so animated when she speaks. "I suppose you haven't been there yet, but we've worked together for years, dear. Practically since the beginning. Darryl here works at the energy plant where your father and grandfather used to work."

I raise my brows, feigning excitement, but to hear someone I don't know speak about my father is beyond awkward.

Darla doesn't seem to notice because she's still talking. "I'm what people here like to call an *Elder*. Darryl, too, of course."

Turns out she's not the only Elder in the room. It seems everyone here plays some grand role in the community. I keep hearing buzzwords and phrases like *unrestricted improvements, renewable energy sources, future installments,* and *the values that govern our society.* Keeping up with all of the lingo is exhausting, but at least I try for the first part of the morning.

In an effort to tune out the town politics for a while, I sneak away to the back corner of the room, where the white grand piano sits. I duck behind it and take a seat on a bench, eager for a break from the celebration.

One thing that lingers in my mind is how everyone I've come across boasts about Rose and her overwhelming contributions to the town. It's hard not to be mesmerized by how she floats around the room, too, never losing her sincerity and grace. The way her laughter sounds like it's tickling the white flower petals that sit atop the piano, she truly is infectious when she's in her environment.

"Do I finally have the privilege of speaking with *the* Katrina Summer?"

My shoulders stiffen at the familiar voice, but I can't ignore the way my heart skips a beat too. I look to my left and find Alec taking a seat beside me on the bench. He stares back at me, his emerald-green eyes swirled with flecks of gold. A flutter builds in my stomach.

"Alec," I say, unable to hide the nerves that work their way into my voice. He may be one of the only familiar faces in the room, but I'm still humiliated that he only asked me to hang out that night because of my grandma. If Iris and Ava ever found out about that, they would spread that rumor around town so fast. "What are you doing here?"

He doesn't hesitate, despite my rudeness. "I guess I crashed your party. My parents received an invitation, though." He looks around. "And apparently, so did the rest of the neighborhood." When he turns back to look at me, he smiles. "I hope you don't mind that I'm here."

Should I admit that I might actually be starting to enjoy my party now? "I guess I'm just confused as to why you're here, if I'm being honest."

He takes in a deep breath and frowns. "I'm sorry for hurting you, but if you think I wanted to hang out with you just because Rose asked me to, you're so wrong. If anything, she gave me the push to do what I already wanted to do. I like you, Kat. And I wanted to be here today to tell you that." He smiles again, this time unleashing a flock of flutters in my chest. "And to tell you happy birthday."

His shoulder brushes my arm, and the way the touch heats my body, he might as well have kissed me. "Thank you." In an effort to distract my emotions, I take a slow sweeping gaze around the room.

"So," Alec says. "Summer solstice celebration, eh?"

A light laugh escapes me. "Now you know I'm not full of it. I told you, Rose is into this stuff." Leaning closer to him, I drop my voice to a whisper. "Maybe Rose will perform some of her witchcraft for us." I give him a wink. My growing boldness doesn't cease to amaze me.

Alec's face twists apologetically. "Man, I've really been coming off like a jerk since we met, huh?"

I shrug jokingly. "A little bit, yeah."

He looks at me now, eyes curious, as if waiting for me to say something more, but Charlotte approaches us. She looks stunning in her gold-and-silver-glittered facemask. Her sky-blue dress is long and flowy. Her short blond hair frames her face in an angled bob. If I didn't know better, I would swear she was sculpted from porcelain.

"Kat, there you are. You disappeared."

I smile up at her. "Yeah, I was starting to fall asleep."

She laughs, then her curious eyes scan Alec. "I don't believe we've properly met." She sticks out a hand. "Alec, is it?"

He takes it while brightening with his charming smile. "That's me. And you're Charlotte."

She nods, looking pleased that he knows. "And your parents are..." She taps a finger to her lips while she searches the party. "There. The professor and his wife. Charlie and Brenda." She snaps as if she's proud of her memory.

"That's them."

"Well," Charlotte says while looking between us. "I'll

leave you two to enjoy yourself." She leaves me with a questioning glance before turning and walking away, and I know it's because she's confused at seeing Alec and me together.

Alec gets me up off the bench and forces me to walk through the party. We head to the refreshment table first. It's adorned with fruit baskets, more flowers, and a sculptured centerpiece of Goddess Hecate, a touch I'm sure Rose is responsible for. I try to ignore Johnny as he replaces an empty tray of fresh strawberries before disappearing into the crowd.

When we get to the end of the long table, Alec grabs two wine glasses and fills them with fruit punch from a three-tiered cement-textured fountain.

I take the drink with a grateful smile. "I've been dreading this day—" My confession catches him off guard, and his face becomes bright with confusion, but a smile still lingers on his face. "Until now."

As expected, Alec relaxes again and even smiles. "Well then, good. I'm glad I came. Even if I did have to crash."

"For what it's worth, I'm glad you did."

"I'm glad you said that because..." He pulls something from behind his back. It's shiny, red, and wrapped with a bow.

"You didn't need to get me anything," I say with surprise, unable to take my eyes from it.

I start to reach for it, then Rose approaches, startling us both. "Alec, I'm surprised to see you here."

He doesn't miss a beat. "I wanted to wish Katrina a happy birthday and to clear up a little misunderstanding we had."

He wraps an arm around my waist and guides me closer. "I think we're square now, aren't we?"

He winks at me, and I know I'm blushing furiously. "We are. We're good."

Rose raises a brow before a hint of a smile plays across her face. "Good. Then that means I'm forgiven too. I was getting quite tired of the cold shoulder, dear."

Alec and I laugh while Rose spots the red box. "Oh, a gift. I'll put that with your other things." After snatching it from his hand, Rose leans in so only I can hear. "You feeling okay?"

What a strange question. I nod, wondering if I appear to be pale or sick. "I feel great." It's the truth.

"Good, good." She darts a look up at the clock then back to me. "Meet me on the beach at noon." Then she walks away like as if that wasn't a strange request.

"What's next, birthday girl?"

My eyes find the floor-to-ceiling windows of the great room, and instantly, I want nothing more than to escape to the outside. I don't even think twice about reaching for Alec's hand and dragging him through the patio entryway.

We stop near the pool, and I release his arm. "Sit with me?"

Before he's even responded, I kick off my heels and sit at the pool's edge. I slide my feet into the water, letting them fall against the wall. Alec has to remove his shoes and roll up his jeans first, but he follows my lead.

"So where are your better halves today?" I tease.

He chuckles. "If you're talking about the dynamic duo that is Iris and Ava, they're shopping."

"And they didn't need you to hold their bags?" I bat my lashes at him jokingly.

"Oh, they did," he teases back. "But I told them I had more important things to do, like get the Summer Girl to forgive me so we can finish what we started during our last swim."

A flashback of our kiss sends a blast of heat through me. "You actually told them that?"

He squishes his face and shakes his head. "No, I left out the details, but this is a small town. They'll figure out who I spent the day with eventually."

I groan. "And then I'm in for it."

Alec chuckles. "No, you won't be 'in for it.' I know those two can be a little much, but they're harmless. They just don't take to new people well, I guess."

I tilt my head. "Didn't you say you moved here not too long ago?"

"Yeah, but I'm a guy. It's different." When I roll my eyes, he gives me a sideways grin. "Besides, they glare at all pretty girls. You should take it as a compliment."

I bite down on my lip. "So you think they'll warm up to me?"

He makes a face. "I hope so, but I was just trying to tell you that I think you're pretty—in case you missed that part."

The comment catches me off guard. I let out a nervous laugh as my pulse quickens. I can't remember the last time a guy called me pretty—especially by anyone as attractive as Alec.

His smile melts me to my toes. "I'm sorry. I guess I'm bad at flirting."

I let out a quiet laugh. "No, I guess I'm just bad at realizing when someone is flirting." The embarrassment lingers. My cheeks are hot, and I know I'm red all over for the millionth time today.

I look in every other direction except at Alec, afraid that if I look into his eyes one more time, he'll see the girl I was back in Silver Lake. The loner. The loser. The weirdo. Up until now, I've done a good job of leading a semblance of a normal life. Maybe it won't be so bad here after all.

He starts to move in, and my breath hitches in my throat. I don't know why I'm a thousand times more nervous than I was before our first kiss, but my heart is hammering, my pulse feels like it's zooming a million miles a minute, and everything feels hot. Too hot.

His fingers twist through mine, then he's pulling me closer and closer, until his lips are nearly touching mine.

A flash of something above catches my eye, and I glance up at my balcony to find whatever was just there is gone. *That was strange.* But I don't have time to think about it long.

"Kat."

My name is just a faint sound, even though I know it's coming from Alec beside me. I shake my head, trying to rid my mind of the strange sensation percolating through my body.

"What time is it?" It's all I can think to ask.

"It's noon," the faint sound responds.

And that's when it happens. It's like I'm not even in control of my own body when my chin lifts. My eyes look up, directly at the sun. I've learned enough about the summer solstice to know that noon on this day is when the sun reaches its highest point. But why does it feel like its rays are pouring through my body, filling me with enough energy to light an entire city?

The sun is too bright. I attempt to look away, but I'm blinded by a brighter, familiar light. It takes over my sight like it did that first day on the beach.

I jam my eyelids together, squeezing them, expecting to drown the bright light with darkness, but it lingers. Just as panic sets in, an electric shock jolts my insides, like a spark igniting every nerve in my body. It's... exhilarating... I think. There's nothing painful about it this time. Nor is there a headache that accompanies the light. All I can feel is the sun infusing me with a heat that reaches my bones.

I try again, slowly opening and closing my eyes as dizziness overcomes me. My head feels foggy, and it's too much to hold on anymore. And then I'm plummeting forward into a deep white cloud of nothingness.

SIXTEEN

The world is moving in slow motion. I open my eyes, but the blinding white light persists, sending me into a panic. My breathing becomes shallow as I try to make sense of my surroundings.

Where am I?

There's sand between my toes, heat is kissing my cheeks, and the faint sounds of a party start to trigger my memory. Then my sight slowly begins to return.

"What the..." I gasp and whirl around. I'm on the beach in front of Summer Manor. The party seems to still be in full swing, but...

How did I get here? I was *just* sitting by the pool with Alec. Confused and disoriented, I fall to my knees just as a shadow of someone approaching appears on the sand. Using my hands to block the sunlight from my eyes, I spot Rose.

She watches me, waiting for me to react as if this is some sort of science experiment and she knows what just happened.

"What was that?" I know my tone is accusatory, but she knows something, and I'm starting to run out of patience.

"How do you feel?"

I look at her, incredulous. "How do I *feel*? I was just sitting by the pool with Alec. There was a bright light, then I was falling. Now I'm here. How do I *feel*? I feel crazy. Do you know what's happening to me? I'm scared, Rose. Something is wrong with me." My voice is shaking.

Rose smiles, which is not at all what I was expecting. "Hush, dear. You're perfectly fine. Alec thinks you wanted some fresh air, so he went inside to wait for you. Now, tell me. Are you feeling okay?"

I want to blurt out that I'm not. How could I feel okay after what just happened? But that's the craziest part of all. I am fine. I'm better than fine. Every nerve ending in my body is buzzing with electricity. My heartbeat is strong and steady within the confines of my ribcage, and I just feel strong— physically and mentally.

"It's beginning." Pure happiness spreads across Rose's face as she mutters those two words that send chills straight up my spine.

"What's beginning?

Rose places her hands on my cheeks. "Welcome to your Enchantment."

Huh? "My what?"

"Your Enchantment. Your becoming. Your... awakening."

No matter how many versions Rose comes up with, I still don't understand.

"It's a wonderful thing, Katrina, I promise you. Don't be afraid of what you're feeling. Embrace it." Rose drops her hands from my face and smiles. "Come with me. We'll cut the cake. When everyone leaves, we'll have a chat."

"Wait. You want the party to be over?"

Rose nods. "We have a lot to talk about. Just don't make a wish when you blow out the candles."

My jaw drops. "This is my birthday party, Rose. That's what people do when they blow out their candles. They make wishes."

"Just trust me, Katrina. All will become clear soon."

Not knowing what else to do, I follow her up the back stairs, past the pool and patio, and through the back entrance of the house. All the guests are now drifting from the room, greeting me as I pass them. I try to smile back.

I spot Alec standing off to one side of the room with his parents. I'm desperate to know what he thinks of all this. Did I really tell him I needed some fresh air? I don't remember that at all. But he looks perfectly happy. When he catches me staring, he smiles back at me with a boyish grin.

I go through the motions for the rest of the party, watching as a three-tiered cake with white frosting and green trim is wheeled into the room. Everyone sings, I blow out the candles, then thunderous applause ensues. For the next hour, the guests start to thin out. Alec is one of the last to leave.

"Thanks for stopping by, Alec. I'm sorry we didn't get a chance to talk much."

He shoves his hands in his pockets and shrugs. "We have plenty of time for that, right? Or do you still plan on leaving Apollo Beach?"

I think about what happened outside. "I think I'll be around for a bit longer than I thought."

His megawatt grin makes me smile too. "Good." He leans

forward to hug me, brushing my cheek with his lips before breaking away. "Happy birthday, Summer Girl."

***

ROSE AND CHARLOTTE are huddled together, sharing a giggle, when I walk back into the great room.

"What the hell is going on?"

Their heads snap toward me, and they freeze while shock lights up their faces. It's not like me to speak that way, but I've been going crazy trying to understand what's going on with me.

Rose's face relaxes, and she gestures to the couch. "Have a seat, Katrina. All will be discussed. But first," she says with a clap of her hands, "presents."

I burst into an incredulous laugh. "What? No. I'm not opening presents. You're going to tell me what's going on." I look at Charlotte, whose eyes are on Rose like she doesn't want to get involved. My eyes narrow at her. "Does she know what's happening too?"

Rose sighs while Charlotte throws me a sympathetic glance. "Charlotte is aware, yes."

"Oh, Rose." Charlotte frowns. "Stop delaying."

Rose raises her arms in a dramatic shrug as if to say she's innocent. "I'm not delaying. This is all part of the reveal. You open your presents, and the pieces will all start to fall together." She gestures again at the couch. "Now, sit."

I feel I have no other choice, so I sit across from Rose. Charlotte proceeds to hand me cards and presents, and the only thing I seem to be learning is just how generous my grandmother's friends are. I open money, gift certificates, lavish bath products, fancy jewelry, and what looks like a handmade quilt. When Charlotte hands me a small shiny red box wrapped with a silver bow, my heart skips. I know exactly who this one is from.

Charlotte and Rose watch as I gently open it to find a sand dollar lying on a velvet cushion. There's a folded piece of paper pressed into the lid. I open it to find a note from Alec.

Summer Girl,

I found this sand dollar on the night we met, and I knew it should belong to you.
Happy Birthday.

Alec

THE GIFT IS SO SWEET, but I can't help but wonder if whatever is happening to me will sabotage the feelings Alec and I have toward one another.

When I look back up from the gift, Charlotte is rolling a bicycle into the room from the foyer. My jaw drops. It's not just any bicycle. It's a white vintage classic retro beach cruiser with thin rubber wheels and silver spokes, much like the one I used to have back in Spring Lake.

"Is that for me?"

Rose grins. "It is. Charlotte and I thought you could use a

little help getting around. You know, until you get your license. Do you like it?"

I cross the room and take the bike by the handlebars, emotion rising in my throat from the unexpected gesture. "Thank you. I love it."

Rose winks at me. "I told you it was a day for magical things, didn't I?"

My head snaps back to hers, then I feel myself start to shake. "Rose, please tell me what happened to me on the beach."

Charlotte takes the bike from me and rolls it away.

Rose gestures for me to come back to the couch, then she leans forward. "Okay, but I have one more present for you, Katrina. A family heirloom that's been in our family for thousands of years. It's a family tradition that you receive this on your eighteenth birthday."

She pulls another gold-wrapped package from behind her back and brings it over to me. I take it slowly. With shaking hands, I unwrap the package to find a long jewelry box. I crack it open, and immediately, I feel faint. Inside is the same green stone from my dream. The one I was wearing as I stared back at my reflection. The same stone I saw in Rose's den. The one she described as a rare green emerald crystal.

"It's beautiful," I say breathlessly, more freaked out by the vision.

The next thing I know, Charlotte is behind me, gently placing the necklace with the ancient stone around my neck. I suck in a slow breath as I sort through the anxious feelings that take hold of my chest.

"What's wrong, Kat?" Charlotte's question is almost expectant, as if she knows the answer.

A tear falls from the corner of each eye, and I swipe them away. "What is going on?" I whisper. "I've spent the past two years wondering why I'm so... different. I get angry and accidents happen, and people look at me like I'm some kind of devil. Ever since I arrived in Apollo Beach, things have only gotten stranger. Why am I having visions and dreams that all feel so real?" I touch the emerald. "Like this. I was wearing it in a dream I had when I first arrived."

I release the necklace and suck in another breath. "But not only that." I think of that day I overheard a conversation from clear across a restaurant. "How can I hear things that I shouldn't?" I think about my endurance when I went for that jog with Alec and how quickly I picked up the game of pool. Sure, all of that could be pure coincidence and good luck, but what if it means something more? "It all seems so impossible."

"It's not." Rose speaks clearly and confidently, and I hang on her every word as if they will decide my future. "I couldn't have possibly prepared you for what you've been experiencing. Your visions, your dreams, your heightened senses, it's all part of something... well, enchanting."

There's that word again. Rose knows she has my attention. I haven't moved. She shifts slightly as if waiting for me to cut in with my questions.

When I say nothing, she continues. "You are an Enchanter, my dear. More specifically, a Solstice. It's what I am too."

I stare at Rose while anger builds up inside me, just

waiting for her to start laughing and tell me this is all a practical joke. "I don't understand what that means."

"It means that we have the power to do great things in this world. Magical things. Everything that is happening to you is directly related to your ancient Greek heritage, but from today on, today being your eighteenth birthday, you are in full control of your powers."

"Powers? Magic?" My eyes narrow. "Do you know how crazy you sound right now?"

Despite my fury, Rose smiles. "Think about it, dear. The accidents that always landed you in hot water—your strength and endurance, your heightened senses—and tell me, have you made any wishes that happened to come true? Those weren't coincidences. All of it is just a small part of what you are capable of. Your dreams and visions are your powers' ways of communicating with you—to warn you, to help you. Don't discount them."

I stare back at her, bewildered, as the image of myself in the vanity crosses my mind again. "I was levitating a vase in my dream, Rose."

Rose shrugs. "Levitation is a power you possess. Try it."

I stand up abruptly, furious with this mad woman I have come to live with. "Stop it. This is not funny. You think I'm seriously going to believe that I have magical powers?" I choke out a laugh. "Rose, I've been through so much lately. The dreams and the headaches are obviously all part of that. You should be encouraging me to see a doctor, not feeding me ridiculous lies." I'm close to tears.

Before I know what's happening, Rose puts up her hand, and something of great force slams into my chest. It reels me back into the couch, which then slides across the floor, only held from careering across the room by Charlotte's grip.

"Rose! Stop it!" Charlotte's voice breaks through my shock and my grandmother's intense stare.

Rose shakes her head as if breaking free from a trance. She's breathing deeply now. "I didn't mean to scare you, Katrina. I just needed you to see."

My heart pounds as I come to grips with what just happened. Rose is now some distance away. I look at Charlotte. "What was that?" I ask meekly.

Rose sighs, and I turn to her. "I did it. It's my magic, but I'm old. I've lost a lot of energy over the years, and over time, things have become harder to control. I try not to practice anymore, for fear of something going horribly wrong. I'm sorry." She seems to calm down quickly and continues. "You've been reading about Greek mythology, yes? I told you about Astina Summer. You've read up on the stories of gods. Is it so hard to believe that we are descendants of those gods?"

I let out a breath. "I suppose not, but those are just *myths*. Do you know what the definition of a myth is? A myth is a *false* belief or idea."

Rose rolls her eyes. "Clearly, you won't believe me until you do it yourself. You just have to try. Try to levitate something." Rose points at the cake on the table. "There."

"Rose, stop." Charlotte scoots closer to me. The authority in her voice surprises me, but her relationship with Rose is another strange aspect that I still don't understand. Since I came here, Charlotte has acted more like a caretaker to me than to Rose. But as grateful as I am to Charlotte for jumping to my defense, I can't believe she's been drinking the Kool-Aid too. Charlotte obviously believes what Rose is saying.

"I think I need to be alone," I croak. "Please. Can I go to my room? Or are you going to stop me again?" I focus on Rose as I speak.

Charlotte turns to face me. "Rose just wants to help you. It's who you are, Kat. You wanted to know why these things are happening to you. I know it all sounds crazy, but it's real." Her smooth-as-silk voice helps, but it's not enough to overcome what I'm seeing and hearing.

I look at her, my eyes wide with annoyance. Then I look at the cake Rose wanted me to levitate. "I won't do it."

Charlotte and Rose exchange a glance, then Charlotte is placing a hand on mine before lifting it in the air. "Here. You aim with your mind. Like it's a wand. Focus on what you want to do, and do it."

As gentle and instructional as Charlotte is, I cannot take her seriously. I don't know whether to laugh or cry. Charlotte releases my hand, leaving me pointing numbly at the cake.

I try to do as she says. I even wiggle my fingers, but I feel ridiculous and lower my hand. "See? I can't do it." I stand. "You two are officially insane. May I be excused?"

Rose nods, disappointment washing over her expression. "You're dismissed."

As I take the grand staircase, I can't help but listen into the conversation below, as clear as a bell. I refuse to believe there's anything magical about my great hearing.

"She needs to see for herself, Rose. Just give her time. It's not like she can escape it."

"That girl is so stubborn," Rose hisses. "Just like her mother."

"Stop it!" Charlotte hisses. "She can probably hear us."

Rose scoffs. "Why would she? She doesn't believe in the power, so she won't believe what she's hearing."

Charlotte sighs. "Give her time."

"We don't have time." Rose's voice sounds dejected and scared. Despite the current situation, my heart grows heavy for the old woman.

What does she mean, *We don't have time?*

I close the door to my bedroom, step in front of my vanity mirror, and reach up to unclasp the green necklace that now weighs heavily on my chest. I hold it in my quivering hands as a sigh leaks through my teeth in a quiet sizzle. I catch the eye of my reflection, which vaguely resembles the young girl who came to live in Apollo Beach just three weeks ago.

I know I've changed during my short time here. My hair has grown, my complexion has cleared and darkened, and my eyes have lightened some. But deep down inside, I know I'm no different than the strange outcast of a girl whose actions could have very well led to her mother's death.

I'm not filled with magic. I'm cursed.

SEVENTEEN

U sing all my strength to pull myself from the darkness, I try to escape the water. The current is as resilient as an anchor. Water rushes over me, slamming me deeper into the murky depths. My body is thrown against a rock just as a large glittery blue fin swims by. I scream, causing water to bubble around me as I use the last of the air in my lungs.

I'm jolted from my sleep and forced to adjust to the morning light. I shudder, feeling as if I'm not alone, like someone was just here watching me. I swivel my head, surveying my surroundings. My suspicions are somewhat confirmed. Someone *was* in my room. The French doors are wide open, allowing the warm morning breeze to float in from the bay.

With a swift kick, I throw off my covers then sit up, senses on high alert. Something tells me the windows haven't been open for long. It only takes a second to spot the green emerald necklace lying on my balcony. I look at my vanity mirror, where I remember placing the necklace last night, then back to the balcony rail. *How did it get there?*

At a snail's pace, I move toward it, heart pounding

rapidly. I say a silent prayer that my imagination has gotten the better of me, most likely triggered by the previous day's events. Up close, I examine the odd-shaped necklace. I know nothing about jewelry, except that this piece is stunning. It glimmers radiantly as the stone's facets catch the sunlight. The imperfections in the long jagged edges are mesmerizing. Lifting it, allowing the gold chain to dangle, I watch the emerald glow once more. The stone doesn't frighten me anymore. I place the chain around my neck because it somehow feels wrong to be without it, and the stone now hangs lightly upon my chest, unlike last night. It's as if my acceptance of the grand jewel makes the weight manageable.

I rest my elbows on the balcony rail, reflecting on the events from the previous day. Rose outdid herself with the elaborate party filled with eccentric costumes, all for my birthday, an occasion she believed to be some sort of *enchanting*. A laugh bubbles up my throat at the ridiculousness of the way she demanded I levitate a cake in front of her and Charlotte. Such utter foolishness.

Discomfort snakes through me when I remember the invisible force that pushed me back and onto the couch so hard that I lost control of my own body. Rose and Charlotte seemed to think Rose caused that, but how is that even possible? There has to be another explanation.

Maybe Rose is the head of a cult. The thought reassures me in a way. It's something that actually makes sense. What doesn't make sense are how some of my visions and dreams have been coming true. That's a chilling realization since last night's dream ended in my death.

My thoughts are interrupted by something far out in the

bay. A boat sails by with two men standing near the bow. They're holding fishing poles, but that's not what sends a shiver through me. I'm able to follow the fishing line that runs from the tip of a pole down into the water.

"Impossible," I say on a hushed breath. The boat has got to be at least a mile away, but my vision is weirdly perfect. More than perfect. It's as if everything is magnified.

I look down the beachfront, and I swear my eyes are playing tricks on me. I scan the houses down the row from ours, unsure what I'm looking for. I'm just searching for some kind of clue that I'm not going crazy—then my eyes lock on a warning label on an electrical box ten houses down. It's blurry at first, but as I begin to focus on it, my sight adjusts to perfection, and I can read it clearly.

I suck in a deep breath and remember what Rose mentioned about heightened senses. Can it be possible that all of my senses are more powerful now? I look down at the beach and spot an elderly couple. They appear to be in mid-discussion as they walk side by side at the water's edge. The voices are amplified the second I focus in on them.

Their conversation is as clear as the water running onto the shore. Their grandchildren are coming into town and staying for a few days while their parents vacation in the Hamptons. The old man wants his wife to stop at the store and get a few things before they arrive. I squeeze my eyes shut and open them again, muting the radio in my head. I scold myself for invading their privacy.

Okay. So my vision is excellent, and my hearing is perfect. I sniff and smell the scent of bacon coming from the kitchen below. That's hardly new. I could smell bacon from across the state if I wanted it badly enough. Is it so hard to believe that I've simply been blessed with strong senses?

As I turn around and lean my back against the balcony rail, my eyes settle on my vanity. I can almost hear the pounding in my chest as a shiver runs down the length of my spine. My inner voice pleads for me to go to it. I move forward shakily and take a seat in front of the mirror. In its reflection, I look beyond my narrow shoulders to where the vase sits on my nightstand. It holds fresh pink flowers, just like it did in my dream. I don't question how they got there or who put them there. None of that seems to matter.

I reach up to gently lift my necklace from my chest. I take a shaky breath then wrap my fingers around it until the entire stone is safely in my grip. I do my best to tune out every sound, thought, and feeling until I'm focused solely on the vase across the room. Then I squeeze the stone, combatting a conversation in my subconscious that tells me I'm being ridiculous for even entertaining my grandmother's theory. Of course I can't make it float in midair.

With a vigorous shake of my head, I force the negative thoughts away and clear my mind. I zoom in on the vase with my eyes until it's in focus and everything around it tilts and blurs. My next mental command is so powerful, my muscles shake in reaction to the tension. Then I watch in astonishment as the vase rises and begins to float in midair.

ROSE IS outside by the pool when I go to look for her later that afternoon.

"You missed breakfast," Rose says, irritation evident in her tone. She reclines on one of the lounge chairs beside the pool, beneath a multi-colored umbrella.

I choose not to speak. Instead, I stare across the pool and lock my eyes on a plant in a large ceramic pot. Seconds later, it rises off the ground, and I will it to move toward us. Rose gasps, and I lose my concentration. The pot falls and splashes into the pool.

I look over at my grandmother, who appears stunned. "I've been practicing."

Her shock turns to glee, then she claps her hands enthusiastically. "Finally." She sits up straight. "How does it feel?"

I'm having trouble finding my words. I didn't exactly prepare for any of this. I'm just going with the flow, hoping something will click. All I know now is that I need to talk to someone, and whether I like it or not, Rose is the best person for that. "I don't know, Rose. This is all so hard to come to terms with."

"I know, dear, but it's in you. It's who you've always been —since birth. Don't you see? You've never been strange or cursed. You've simply been becoming what you were always meant to be. You've got to see that now. That there's been something in you just begging to be released?"

I can't argue with her there. Then something clicks, and I have to ask, "Did my mom know about all of this?"

Rose nods, her eyes never leaving mine. "It's why she kept you away, Katrina. She didn't want you to become—" She sweeps a hand up and down, gesturing to all of me. "But there was no stopping it."

"You spoke about divine intervention before. Are you

saying that because she tried to keep me away from all of this, from you and from Apollo Beach, that it ended up killing her?"

Rose tilts her head, and I can see she's trying to find the right words. "I believe so, yes."

Sorrow fills me to the brim. "So, what now?"

"You embrace it," Rose says. "You learn, you train, and then you find out how to exist in a world that desperately needs you."

I take a few more steps to get to the lounge chair beside her and sit. "But why would the world need any of this? Nothing good has come from what I'm capable of."

"That's because you didn't know what you possessed. We start to feel the effects of our Enchantings months, sometimes years, before we officially get our powers. That's when the magic inside of us comes alive. Yesterday, on your eighteenth birthday, under the high sun of the summer solstice, your transformation was complete. That's why at the moment noon hit, you could no longer hide from what you are."

"Why didn't you try to warn me?"

Rose shakes her head. "Oh no, dear. It's Solstice law to not discuss one's Enchantment until full development is reached. There are some exceptions to the rule, but the law book states that I had to wait."

"There's a Solstice law book?"

"There is. You'll come to know it well. You'll also learn to control when and how your powers are used. Trust me, Katrina. You've been bestowed such an incredible gift."

"By who?"

"Many years ago, dating back to a time that is untraceable, as far as our family history goes, a goddess was born on the day of the summer solstice."

"Astina Summer," I say on a breath.

Rose smiles. "That's right. Astina, the Goddess of Enchantment, is the original summer solstice goddess. Before the Horae existed, Astina came to be the most powerful goddess of our seasons. She was said to have grown to be a magical being with powers only to be used for the good of mankind. As Astina grew into her power, people did not fear her. They were captivated by her beauty and magic, and indeed, she only used her powers for good. Her Followers believed she was the purest soul on earth, and that her powers were bestowed to her because of that goodness. Her Followers strived to live a life as pure as her—to help others, to be generous—and as a thank you, they were gifted powers of Enchantment as well."

I swallow. "So that's it? That's how the Summer bloodline began?"

"Almost, dear. When Astina was set to marry, she wished for an opposite to complete her, to help her carry on the bloodline of the solstice. She met two men, one of whom would turn out to be her Fated, her one true mate. The other, her nemesis for a lifetime to come."

I shudder, but continue listening without a word.

"Her Fated was Zavier, another primordial god, who had been born on the day of the winter solstice. They grew together and created a family that commenced your bloodline—their children, the descendants of their power. Your grandfather, your father, and you are direct descendants of that blood."

I frown as hundreds of questions form at once. "But what about you? Does that mean you haven't always been a Solstice?"

Rose smiles. "I have. I come from a line of original Followers, those who were gifted Solstice powers by Astina. After Astina passed away, the ability to grant Enchantment died. We can, however, become Enchanted Solstices through marriage. We can also invite new Followers in to partake in our events and witness our actions. It's one way we keep ourselves in check."

My mind is spinning. "So there are Solstices, Followers, and—" I look up at her. "What do you call someone who doesn't possess powers and who isn't let in on the secret?"

"They are called Normals."

"Normals." I say the word quietly, as if I might offend someone.

Rose smiles. "It's not an insult, Katrina. We all coexist, but our purposes are different."

I swallow. "So, then what about my mom? Was she a Normal until she married my father? You said she knew what you all were."

Rose hesitates for a second before responding. "Grace wasn't brought into the secret until after she married Paul. She had to wait until she was officially Enchanted before she could be let in on our secrets. Like I mentioned, it is Solstice law not to disclose who we are to anyone else. Since she wasn't a Follower, she had to wait."

"That's a little confusing."

Rose nods. "As is any law, I suppose. But it exists to protect our kind from danger."

A chill shakes through me. "Danger?"

"At the start of our existence, Astina grew to be an all-powerful goddess with thousands of Followers, both Enchanted and not. There was another—an opposite—who became jealous of Astina's powers."

"Wait. You said there was a second opposite when she was to choose her Fated. Is that who you're referring to now?"

Rose nods. "Yes, the God of Darkness, Erebus. You see, there were two other primordial gods that came to be around the same time as Astina and Xavier. The God of Autumn and the Goddess of Spring. Together, they created an Equinox bloodline that worked and lived parallel to the Solstice bloodline. But the God of Darkness became jealous of what they were creating. He murdered the primordial Equinox Gods and created an army out of the Equinox descendants to rival Astina. Out of fear, the Equinox did as Erebus commanded to work against her, doing whatever they could to sabotage her position of leadership in the deity community. Erebus and his Followers caused the Great Enchanted War in ancient Greece in an attempt to over-throw Astina completely. Loved ones were torn apart, our bloodlines were compromised, and while the Solstice Army came out on top, the Equinox Army still exists to this day."

Fear bristles in my chest. "Are you serious?"

"Quite serious, dear. The threat is real, but we've built a safe community around the world, one that thrives by constructing protections all around us. While Zeus created the Horae to preside over the seasons and time, it never changed our roles, even if the Greek mythology stories don't reflect our history." She purses her lips to reflect her annoyance. "As Solstice descendants, we believe in the purest of all things. We do not tolerate evil, sinning, or defiance of any kind. Our ancestry tells us that the purer our souls are, the stronger our powers grow to be. And that is how we live."

For eighteen years, I've lived in a world where magic was make-believe and Greek gods and goddesses were merely elaborate stories told as a way of teaching, and here she is, expecting me to accept this as if it's all real.

"I'm sorry, Rose, but so much of this isn't adding up. If we are good, why would my mom take me away?"

"Oh, Kat—" Rose's expression falls, revealing her age. She sees my impatience and places a hand on my shoulder. "You will know everything, I promise, but there's a lot you need to understand first."

I should have known the secrets wouldn't stop. It seems Rose is filled with them. I push my frustration aside for the time being. "Are there many others?"

Rose's eyes light up. "Oh, yes. Some live here, in Apollo Beach. You'll meet them all soon."

"What about Charlotte? Is she a Solstice too?"

"She is." Rose adjusts herself in her chair. "Charlotte lost her parents many years ago. Like you and your mom, she was left without parents at a very young age. She's traveled the world, alone with her power and a vague understanding of her existence."

My heart squeezes. "That's so sad."

"You'll find it's actually a common occurrence in our community."

I tilt my head but say nothing, allowing Rose to complete her train of thought. At least she's talking.

"Over the centuries, our kind has been split apart by wars and circumstances beyond our control. Some descendants live their entire lives without knowing what they are or how to control what they can do. Settlements were established around the world to keep whatever communities we could together. One of those settlements is here, in Apollo Beach. Solstices are drawn here like moths to a flame."

"That's amazing."

"It is. Out of all things I do here, my favorite thing is to help the Lost find out where they came from. Some stay, and some leave. That's how Charlotte found me, and I'm so grateful that she stayed. She's been a wonderful companion to me ever since George... well—" Her voice catches. "Anyway, I'm used to the Solstice life, but since his death, my powers only grow weaker with age. A direct descendant's powers are much stronger, and they can survive a longer lifespan."

"So one day your powers will just fade completely?"

There's a darkening in her eyes that twists in my gut. "Something like that, yes."

I frown, her answer not sitting well with me. "So, what is it that we can do exactly?"

"As Enchanters, we can manipulate the natural progression of things. We can even influence the emotions and sometimes the actions of others. What we can't do is rewrite history."

"But we can levitate and teleport?"

Rose chuckles. "Levitate, yes. Teleport, not exactly."

I frown, confused. "But then how do you explain what happened to me yesterday? One second I was at the pool with Alec, and then next, I was on the beach alone."

"We call that cross-dimensional awareness. It's when your senses take over your body and allow you to travel between two planes of existence. When I came outside and saw you with Alec, I saw what was happening. I immobilized him so he wouldn't see. Then I planted a little scenario in his mind before releasing him from the frozen state." She shrugs like there was nothing strange about it at all. "He walked inside, none the wiser, and I went to the beach to find you."

"Wow."

She allows me to process the information for some time before she perks up. "Now that you know I'm not crazy." She smiles. "What do you say we get started on your training?"

A wild fluttering sensation comes alive in my stomach. I don't know if I'll ever be ready for this, but I follow Rose into the house, past the great room, and down to the library.

Once we're inside, she takes me up a set of stairs and grins at me from over her shoulder. "You know how there are always secret rooms in old libraries? All you have to do is turn the candlestick?" She places her hand on a wall candle and pulls it forward.

A door doesn't rotate on a mechanical floor as I expect, nor does one flip upside down to reveal a new wall. Instead, Rose literally pulls open a hinged door. She laughs, watching my shocked expression.

Beyond it is another den, this one filled with loose

papers, uneven stacks of books lying about, and another bookshelf stuffed with ragged books of all shapes and sizes. An old desk stands on the far side of the room.

Charlotte sits at it, a titanic-sized book beneath her crossed forearms as she beams up at me. "Hello, Kat. I see you've come to your senses—quite literally, I suppose."

Without answering right away, I sweep the room with my eyes again. A line of photos hangs on one wall, and I stand before them, fascinated. I already know who they are— direct descendants of the Summer Solstice. The first is a hand-drawn illustration of the Goddess of Enchantment, Astina Summer. I stare at her, scrutinizing every detail of her features and soaking them into my memory like I did with her statue.

"I'm still unsure what to make of all this." I'm breathless as my gaze floats across the room and lands on Charlotte.

"If you'll excuse me, Katrina. I will have my afternoon tea now," Rose exclaims. "We will chat later, but for now, Charlotte has everything you need to get started."

I watch her go, still reeling from everything she's told me.

"Sit," Charlotte says, interrupting my thoughts.

And if that wasn't enough to get my attention, a loud scraping against the floor does the trick. When I turn to see what the noise was, I find a chair sliding from the other side of the den. Before I can react, it hits the back of my legs, tipping me back into the chair. I gasp, and Charlotte giggles like a schoolgirl. For the first time this morning, I start to feel relaxed.

"How long have you known about me?" It's the first question out of my mouth, although it's not the first question I want to ask.

Charlotte smiles. "Well, it wasn't too long after I met Rose. I figured it out for myself after knowing you existed." Her face relaxes, expressing her sympathy. "How are you doing with all of this?"

I struggle to find my words. "It's like I know these things are happening, so it's undeniable, but there's still a part of me waiting to wake up from a dream."

"I understand that feeling all too well." Charlotte makes a face. "Imagine these things happening to you and not understanding a thing for ten years. I can't believe I survived as long as I did. I thought I was going crazy, but deep down, I knew there had to be others out there."

Poor Charlotte. "I'm so glad you found Rose."

She smiles. "Me too. And now," she says with a wink, "it's time for me to pay it forward and to help you find your way. Consider me your private tutor."

For the first time since learning about all of this, I allow myself to feel excited about it. "I can't believe we're really talking about practicing magic."

Her smile softens as she leans in to reach for my hand. She squeezes it. "Well, start believing it. Your powers will be out of this world."

I let out a nervous laugh. "You don't know that."

Her smile falls completely, and her eyes widen with a seriousness that grips my heart. "But I do. You're a direct descendant. That's a big deal."

"Rose mentioned that, but that makes me no different than my father and my grandfather."

Charlotte laughs like I've just told her the most amusing story. "Oh, Kat. You have no idea just how rare you are. Not just among the Solstice community, but the Enchanter community as a whole."

"Wait." I frown. "There's a difference?"

Charlotte's laugh deepens. "The Solstices are just one species among the Enchanted gods, but as for you, let me put it this way. It is extremely rare to be born from Astina's bloodline *and* to have your Enchantment on the day of the summer solstice." She squeezes my hand again as if she can't contain her excitement. "Your connection to Astina Summer is by far the strongest connection our kind has ever witnessed." She sits back in her chair, her energy practically buzzing through the air.

I let my breath out in a whoosh. "Geez. No pressure there."

She smiles. "What do you say we get to work?"

EIGHTEEN

"I need a break," I say before slamming the Solstice law book closed.

Dust particles float up into the air, and I wave my hand through them before meeting Charlotte's high-browed stare. "You've barely made a dent in that thing."

I look down at the 3,456-page textbook and balk. "I've read over six hundred pages just today. And it's all written in cursive. My vision is blurring. I'm more of a hands-on learner. I thought you were going to be showing me how to use my powers." I omit the part about how my mind keeps returning to Alec. Guilt compounds with every intercepted call and visit to our front door, but Rose has been adamant about me lying low.

Charlotte presses her lips together like she's trying to contain her amusement. "You heard Rose. You won't be practicing any magic until you've read the entire book."

I push the book away and stand up to stretch. "Fine, then I need to take a break and go for a run or something. Being cooped up in this little room has me all wound up."

Charlotte frowns. "You know how Rose feels about you leaving the house right now. We have a lot of work to do."

"But it's been a week," I whine. "No offense, but this is boring."

I glance at Charlotte just as she finishes her eye roll. "I assure you, there is nothing boring about what we are. Just you wait."

Wait. That feels like all I've been doing. Meanwhile, I have so much energy inside me, I feel like I'm going to burst. It's not just my powers I need to learn about. There are changes happening to my body too. Physical changes. And right now, my inner self feels like a jailed bird that yearns to open its wings. I suck in a deep breath, knowing that my thoughts are only contributing to the compounding firestorm locked inside me.

Charlotte narrows her eyes on me. "Keep reading, and then *maybe* I'll give you a small break."

The fact that the chapter I just finished was over two hundred fifty pages of a variety of powers doesn't help my situation. There seem to be an infinite number of powers to learn, but Rose is adamant that I learn about the protective ones first, like shield manipulation, deflection, and intangibility.

"You're telling me I can prevent a weapon from harming me by allowing it to pass through my body?" I asked Charlotte earlier after reading a small passage on intangibility.

She laughed heartily before correcting me. "An actual weapon? No. Our magic doesn't make us invincible, Kat. If anything, it makes us a target. The book is referring to elemental damage caused by charges of energy."

After realizing Charlotte has already settled back into her own book, I sigh and look back down at the next chapter of Solstice law titled "Restrictions." When I catch myself reading the same passage multiple times, my eyes start to roam around the room until they lock on a candlestick near the door. It's currently dimmed to its lowest light setting. Curious if what I learned about fire manipulation is possible, I narrow my eyes on the flame. Focusing all my energy on the flickering light, I start to widen my eyes again, silently commanding the flame to adjust with my gaze. The flame grows larger, causing excitement to rush through me. I'm already craving to do it again. But when I narrow my gaze, the flame dims.

"Katrina!" Charlotte says with a gasp.

I jump and turn my focus away from the light, but not before the flame blazes back to life so fast and out of control that the glass casing around it explodes.

"Oops." I cringe and snap my gaze to Charlotte, who stares back at me, appearing mortified.

"What are you doing?"

I sit back in my chair and raise my hands. "I told you, I'm going stir-crazy in here."

Charlotte frowns before she starts to use her magic to clean up the shards of glass. She doesn't touch a thing, yet it all sweeps into a nice tidy pile in midair then moves gracefully over to the trash.

"No magic," she says again, this time looking angry. "You're lucky this is all the damage you did. You're only just beginning, Kat, but you should know that every power has a consequence if misused. Solstice law is there for a reason, and there are serious consequences for mishandling the powers you've been given."

Guilt swarms my chest. "I'm sorry. Even before I knew what all of this was, running helped me let off some steam. I think it will help me now too. Please, Charlotte. Give me one hour, then I'll come right back here and pick up where I left off."

Her gaze softens, then she lets out a sigh. "Okay, but take your bike, will you? It's been collecting dust for the past week."

With a squeal, I jump up and throw my arms around her. "Thank you, thank you. I'll be good, I promise."

I'm flying down the steps of the library when I hear her yell, "You have one hour, Kat!"

By the time I free my bike from the garage, I can already feel the release from being bottled up for the past week. I don't have a plan. I don't know where I want to go. I just want to ride and feel the wind on my face as I expel some of this energy inside me.

I'm struck by an overwhelming sense of fulfillment as I pedal around the neighborhood. As the sun hits my face, a complete sense of euphoria washes over me. A gentle breeze sweeps through my hair, and I giggle.

Late June seems to bring a new world to Apollo Beach. Now that it's officially summer, the heat is in the high nineties, but I find myself unbothered by what I used to find an intolerable mix of humidity and heat.

After I've circled the neighborhood a few times, I come to the entrance of the public beach and head straight toward it. I push through, fighting the sand's resistance and laughing into the wind. Flying by the bay-facing homes, I'm consumed by thoughts of everything I've been through lately.

When I near Alec's house, I see him sprawled out in a lounge chair on his pool deck. Knowing he hasn't yet seen me, I slow and hop off my bike as I approach. I'm practically standing beside him when his mouth turns up into a smile.

"Well, there she is. I was wondering if I'd ever see you again."

I smile back, suddenly feeling shy. His arms are bent and clasped behind his head, and his body wears a natural tan like he's been sunbathing just like this all week long. Then I look around, half expecting Iris and Ava to pop out from nowhere. "You alone?"

His smile widens. "Not anymore. Sit with me." He pats the seat beside him.

"Okay," I say with a slight note of hesitation. "But only for a few minutes. I promised Charlotte I wouldn't be out long." I lie back in the chair.

He chuckles. "Ah, now I get why you've turned away all my calls and visits. You're a prisoner."

If only he knew how close to the truth that was. Heat rises up my neck as a pang hits my chest. "I haven't been turning you away. That's all Rose." I've already thought about this lie, but actually letting the words roll off my tongue is harder than I thought. "I told you how I'm finishing up school virtually this summer. Well, the truth is, I didn't exactly leave my last school on the best note. I got into some trouble, and my mom had pulled me out to homeschool me. She died before we ever got a chance to start, and I have quite a bit of catching up to do."

Alec reaches out and squeezes my knee. "I'm sorry to hear all that."

"It's okay. I've already been officially accepted into the School of Gaia in the fall, so it's not too bad."

He sits up straight, slipping off his sunglasses, and his face brightens like a ball of sunshine. "Really? So you're staying in Apollo Beach for good?"

I shrug, not wanting to promise too much when I haven't even thought it out myself. "I'm staying for now." I smile. "But it wouldn't suck hanging out with you while I'm still here."

He scoots off his seat and onto mine, then he cups my chin between his fingers and tilts his head. "There's something different about you." His head is so close to mine, I can smell his minty breath. "I can't figure out what, but I like it."

I look down, wondering if he's referring to what my Enchantment did for me. As Rose and Charlotte explained, there's a new type of energy running through my veins, one that supplies me with the best source of nourishment my body needs to survive in its healthiest state. That's why my hair and eyelashes have grown longer. Even my skin is blemish free, and my eyes appear brighter.

"Never mind," Alec says. "I figured it out."

I look back up at him, catching his gaze dipping down to my lips then back up to my face.

"It's your confidence. You've come a long way from the new girl who ran away from me on the beach a month ago."

I laugh, but something in his expression makes me stop

—a seriousness in his eyes I can't quite escape. Then he's leaning in and pressing his mouth to mine like it's the most natural thing in the world.

"Go out with me," he murmurs against my lips. "Tonight."

I pull back slightly to see his face. "Like a date?"

He raises his brows. "Yes, like a date. Just you and me this time."

My chest aches just at the thought of telling him no, but there's no doubt Rose will throw a fit if I even try to step foot outside of the house again. "I can't. Not tonight."

He frowns. "Then when?"

"You're still having that Fourth of July party, right?"

"Yeah, but that's a week from now. Seriously, Kat? It's summer. It's time to get out of that old manor and see the town. And whatever happened to that job you were going to get at Island Grille."

I cringe just thinking about the reason I never got past my audition. *Johnny.* I've tried to push all thoughts of him away since my party. "It doesn't matter. I'm busy now anyway. Maybe I'll try to talk to Roy when I'm done with school."

"Fine," Alec says. "Fourth of July, it is. And then I can take you on a real date."

I lean in, brushing my lips across his. "Deal." I pull myself away and stand. "I need to get back."

"I'll walk you."

He starts to stand, but I panic and put my hand out to stop him. I don't touch him, but he's flying back down onto the lounge chair.

"Whoa, that was weird." He laughs. "I swear I haven't had a thing to drink."

My heart starts to triple its speed. This is exactly why Rose and Charlotte wanted me to stay home. I have no idea what I even did to cause Alec to fly backward like that.

"Maybe it's the sun," I say, hoping my voice doesn't give away my rattling nerves. "Don't worry about it. I brought my bike here, anyway."

He nods. "All right. Seven o'clock on the Fourth. Don't be late, Summer Girl."

OF COURSE ROSE doesn't agree with my wish to go to Alec's Fourth of July party. We've been arguing about it ever since I got home from my bike ride an hour ago.

"Rose, it's the Fourth of July. Everyone will be there. I really want to go. You don't think I'll have learned a thing or two in the past week?"

Rose sighs. "You'll learn a great deal by then, but we can't be sure how much control you have over your powers. It's just not safe."

"What could happen?"

"A lot could happen."

"Like what? Tell me. Help me understand." I cross my arms.

"I don't know. Maybe you'll accidentally use your powers like you did back in Silver Lake. Accidents can happen when you're being reckless."

"Reckless? Maybe if you'd actually teach me something

instead of forcing me to read all about it, then my magic wouldn't seem so *reckless*."

Rose lets out a breath. "Maybe so. But even then, you are a rare Solstice. Your powers are sure to grow more powerful than anything we've ever seen. It's best to take it slow and play it safe for now."

A new sensation overtakes me—a determination stemming from a lifetime of untold truths. "I'm going to the party, Rose. While I appreciate everything you've done for me and all that you're teaching me, I don't need your permission."

Charlotte looks at Rose while placing a gentle hand on her arm. "She will only be a minute away. If something were to happen, we could step in. Until then, we teach her all that we can."

There's a dark cloud over Rose's expression, one she doesn't even attempt to hide. And after a simple nod of agreement, she stands and gives us both one final look.

But when she turns and begins the retreat to her quarters, the words she speaks so faintly ring loudly between my ears. "You've been warned."

NINETEEN

Three more days of "lockdown" have passed, and I'm itching to get out of the house for another accidental run-in with Alec, even though I know it's out of the question. Rose promised to stop screening my calls if I would heed her warnings and not leave the house again until Alec's party—after I've had some hands-on training. I agreed. So tonight is the night—my first true lesson. And I can't shake the nervous flutters from my belly.

"Hey, Kat, you ready?" Charlotte asks from the hallway outside the open doors of my bedroom.

I stare up at her from where I sit at my vanity and suck in a deep breath before smiling. "Ready as I'll ever be." I reach for my emerald necklace and place it around my neck, nearly missing the concerned look Charlotte gives me.

"Do you take your necklace off often?"

I look at it in the mirror then shrug. "Every night before bed and before I shower. I don't want to ruin it."

Charlotte stands behind me, staring back at our reflection. "This stone isn't what gives you powers, but it's the best tool you have when it comes to controlling what's inside you." She reaches out and lifts the stone from my neck, causing it to glow a vibrant shade of green. "Your emerald is like your wand. You don't need to wave it around, but it circulates energy the way your veins recycle blood. Its power is only useful to whom it is designated, and it works with your natural energy. The power it emits will balance you in a way that is most useful to your mind. Take your dreams, for example—the fire, the drowning. You're still having them, yes?"

I swallow then nod.

"Wear this tonight. You'll see that your dreams won't come."

"But what if my dreams are trying to tell me something? Maybe I should be learning from them. Everything else I envisioned seems to be coming true."

Charlotte nods. "Perhaps. But if your dreams are premonitions, then those events are set in stone. Is it possible to alter the chain of events to prevent certain things from happening? Sure, but that is extremely hard to do. We don't know what triggers one thing to lead to another. The only way you can truly prepare is by learning to harness what's inside you." Charlotte smiles. "Come. Let's eat, and then we'll get back to work, shall we?"

Rose is already in the dining room when we enter. "Pizza's here," she says with a lift of her hand. Two greasy pizza boxes float in midair. Their lids open just as a paper plate flies toward me like a saucer. I'm laughing as I catch it.

I love watching Rose like this—playful and freely using her magic. From what she told me before, she doesn't use it often. "You're using magic," I say as I take a seat. "I thought it made you tired."

Rose nods. "Yes, well, it depends on my mood. That's the best way to explain it. Under true strains of stress, magic takes much more energy to release. But on pizza night"—she winks as a slice with pepperoni floats to her plate—"it's as easy as breathing."

I don't know why this simple fact relaxes me greatly, but it does. I start to reach for the pizza box floating nearest to me when Charlotte cuts in.

"Wait." She looks at Rose. "Should we show Katrina how we eat pizza?"

Rose smirks. "No need to get your hands dirty, dear." She nods. "I think you're ready for your first hands-on lesson."

My eyes grow wide with excitement.

"Now, Kat, pay close attention. This is how Enchanters eat pizza." Charlotte looks to be showing off as she places her hands behind her back and a slice of pizza rises from the box and makes its way to her mouth. After she takes a bite, it drops onto her plate, and she grins. "And that's how it's done."

Rose claps her hands in glee, and I can't help but smile too. "You try now, Katrina. Take a bite."

I concentrate. Luckily, levitation is something I already know how to do, but controlling it has me working harder than I expected. After it hits my cheek, my forehead, and my chest, I get frustrated. "What am I doing wrong?"

"It's a balance thing, dear." Rose nods, signaling for me to try it again. "Imagine your mind is your hand."

The hint Rose gives me helps tremendously. I finally get the slice to my mouth so I can take my first bite. *Heaven.*

"So, how does all of this work in the day-to-day? Are we supposed to chant? And what about spells? Do I have to learn any new languages?" I make a face. "Latin seems as if it would be difficult to master, but I haven't read about anything like that in the Solstice law book."

Rose gives a simple shake of her head. "There are no magic potions or cauldrons. We do not cast spells or speak Latin. We are descendants of gods who call upon and manipulate nature with our minds. You asked me about Wiccans before, and now I can fully answer you. Wiccans believe in many of the same things we do. We both celebrate the gods. The one main difference between Wiccans and Enchanters is that Wiccans call upon their gods to fulfill their requests, while we simply are that magic. You see, our ancestors have given us power to use at our own free will."

"So we're like witches."

Rose shrugs like the term doesn't bother her in the least. "That's just a term, though often not the most appropriate one. We are magical beings who possess power and supernatural abilities, but over time, the term *witch* has come to mean something much more negative than how it originated. I prefer the terms *Solstice* or *Enchanter.*"

I'm still processing Rose's words when we've finished dinner and she proclaims that we're ready for the second lesson. She takes us out to the pool deck, where slow-moving clouds shield the night sky. We make our way around the giraffe-tiled deck to the balcony that faces our private beachfront. I look to my left and right at the proud faces of Rose and Charlotte as they smile out into the bay breeze. It's contagious. I'm smiling now too.

Rose places her hand in mine, and I'm shocked by the touch. Rose and I don't touch like this. Her fingers feel long and smooth, but her grip is tight. I can sense our powers connect, from the palm of my hand to my inner core. Solstice to Solstice. Energy surges through me, and I grow stronger and stronger as the seconds pass. The tingling sensation at the tips of my fingers and toes go away, but the energy in me continues to run through my nerves like an electric current. My mind and body are ignited.

As our energy unites, I'm aware of a drastic change in the sky. The dark looming clouds pick up pace and part as thunder claps, and rain starts to fall. My first instinct is to run, but Rose's grip on my hand is locked tight.

Her smile grows into jubilant laughter as the rain soaks through our clothes, and I can't help but wonder if she's causing it. My hair thrashes around me in response to the wind, but I don't care. Our energy is impenetrable. The power surging through me awakens something new in me— something that hints at unbelievable things to come.

"Take Charlotte's hand," Rose shouts over the wind.

I look at Charlotte. Her hand is extended toward me, but her eyes are closed, and she looks as if she's experiencing something profound. Her chin is raised to the sky as she soaks in the night's energy. I take her hand and face forward, eager to know what Rose will do next. I've never seen her so carefree, so spontaneous.

"Our earth's elements energize us and stimulate our power," she yells over the wind. "We have power without it, but with it, we are that much stronger and that much more in control." Rose continues to shout, raising her voice over the vicious wind.

"Are you doing this?" I shout back, nervousness creeping into my voice. The wind is strong enough to carry us away, but I feel rooted to my spot.

Rose chuckles. "*We* are doing this, Katrina. Together, our power is stronger. It's time you see what we can really do." She pauses for a second then lets out a sound like she's hushing the wind. "Shhh."

In that moment, all grows silent. I look toward the sky. The clouds have vanished. I look out at the calm bay waters, then the moon glows, as if someone is playing with the brightness control. The loudest sound comes from the confines of my ribcage, where my heart still thunders.

Amazing.

"What was that?" I ask, still searching for a hint of the magic I just experienced.

"Environmental manipulation," Charlotte says. They are the first words she's spoken since we've been out here. I'd almost forgotten she was with us.

"I want to show you one more thing." Rose lets go of my hand and steps aside a little. "Energy sourcing is how we reenergize. Just us being out here and taking in all the earth offers is filling our needs as Enchanters, but it's more than that." She looks to Charlotte. "Show her, dear."

Charlotte nods and faces forward. She closes her eyes, fists clenched tight, and takes a slow, deep breath. When she exhales, a fog escapes from her mouth. It circles in front of her, but never vanishes. Charlotte opens her eyes and holds her palm up, careful not to touch the eerie vapor substance. She blows on it gently, and I watch as it transforms into sprinkles of glittery particles that release into the air. The wind comes along, and the particles spread until I can no longer see them.

"That's our power, made up of the earth's elements. What we take from the earth, we give back. It's a cycle of life that keeps us powerful and healthy. That's why when you get to my old age, it's difficult to keep up, but it's up to you how long you choose to recycle. What makes us most powerful can also kill us."

Again, Rose is being vague. I sigh inwardly, but I'm understanding more. I then think about her last sentence. "So what happens when you stop energy sourcing?"

Rose gives me a heartening smile as she says the two most ominous words I think I'll ever hear. "I die."

TWENTY

Some nights, I feel like I'm trapped in a bottle, rattling around, hoping it will tip over and crack, just so I can steal a sip of air from the outside world. It's a bit dramatic, I know, considering I'm currently standing on the massive balcony outside my lavish master bedroom.

Sleep seems impossible lately. Between all the energy racing through my veins, straight to my heart, and the questions that never quit, I'm going out of my mind. And ever since the other night when Rose showed me how to energy source, I haven't been able to get her words off my mind.

What we take from the earth, we give back. It's a cycle of life that keeps us powerful and healthy.

It's all so fascinating how we're able to recycle the earth's elements to enhance our senses and turn our strengths into magic. What I once thought was a strange and terrifying curse feels so different to me now. It feels... like magic. It's also terrifying. To know that one day my end will come—not because of old age, but because I'll choose to take my last breath—that's not a power I want to possess.

Restless, I climb onto the balcony rail and walk the ledge

like it's a tightrope. While I pace back and forth, I consider how high I am from the ground and whether I could make the jump. It's tempting, but I latch on to the trellis beside my balcony, descend a bit, then jump when I'm halfway down, enough to test the strength of my legs from a position no Normal could land carefully.

The second before I hit the patio, I tense to absorb some level of shock. Instead, I just feel like I jumped in place. My laugh carries into the wind, and I look around at the dim house lights and consider my next move. I either abide by Rose's wishes and get back inside, or I take a quick jog to release some of this energy. The thought of maybe running into Alec crosses my mind, and that's enough to tip me over the edge.

A little run won't hurt anybody. With a quick wave of my hand, my tennis shoes tip over the edge of the balcony. I slip them on then tighten the laces, and away I go. I'm jogging along the shore, frowning when there's no sign of Alec by the time I fly past his house. Still, I decide to keep going and run the length of the shore until I get to the public beach then past the abandoned north side of town toward the bridge that cuts through the nature preserve.

As soon as the wildlife cloaks me from the eyes of any Normals who might be around, I speed up to a sprint, letting my feet carry me as far and as fast as I can go. I recognize the path and know I'm close to reaching the end. The view of the energy plant looms ahead when a dark hooded figure rounds the final bend.

My heart lurches the moment I see him. First, I wasn't expecting to see anyone out here at this time of night.

Second, I don't need to see the figure's face to know exactly who he is.

I slow my sprint to a jog then a walk, and he does the same. Neither of us stop until we're a mere six feet from each other. He swipes the hood from his head and glares back at me. While I still have tons of energy, I'm surprised to find myself breathing heavily. I've even managed to produce a small amount of sweat.

"A little late for you to be frolicking around, isn't it?"

It might be dark out, but I'm not oblivious to the way he runs his gaze over my black sports bra and spandex shorts. Annoyed by his casual perusal, I glare. "You talk a lot for someone who has nothing nice to say."

His chuckle is so light and surprising that I almost don't believe it came from him. "So much animosity." He gives a small shake of his head. "You should be careful with that."

I take a step forward to let him know I accept his challenge. "What do you know?"

He takes a step toward me. "I know that only someone out of their goddamn mind would go running out here after midnight. Why does it seem like you're always looking for trouble?"

My mouth falls open. "Did anyone tell you the longer you stare, the harder it is to decipher the truth?"

His mouth tips up at the corner. "Never heard that one before, but I don't have to look at you to know you're up to something."

"Well, I'm not."

"Why is that so hard to believe?"

I shrug as sarcasm drips through my veins. "Maybe

because you're an egotistical prick who can't see past the angry wall he erects. Ever think of that?"

His jaw ticks, and I know my words stung. I wish I found pleasure in returning his jabs. I wish I could stop caring completely. But there are things about Johnny Pierce I'm desperate to understand, starting with his hatred for me.

"Yeah, well, at least I don't bring trouble everywhere I go."

I scoff. "Is that the real reason why you didn't call me after my audition? Because you think I'm trouble? You keep saying it, so you must believe it."

Johnny shrugs. "Not sure you've given me much else to go on. What does it matter anyway? The Grille isn't the only job on the island. Go ask that grandma of yours to get you hired somewhere else."

I can feel my jaw bulge with the grinding of my teeth. While I know he's right, that isn't how this is supposed to work. He has no reason to refuse me the job besides the unwarranted hatred he feels. "How old are you, anyway?" I ask.

His brows bend together as he searches my eyes. "Twenty-two. Why?"

I take another step forward so I'm directly beneath his gaze. "Just what I thought. The body of a man and the personality of a toddler."

He leans down, anger flashing in the blue eyes, which are now pinned on mine. "Looks can be deceiving, can't they, Kat?"

"You could say that." My insides are shaking, my neck

burning from the confrontation. I don't even know what we're talking about anymore.

"Go home." This time his words are just a raspy whisper, but it does something to my insides. My eyes fall closed while my heart takes off with a frantic flutter. I open them again and suck in a deep breath. "I'll go home when I'm done with my run."

He narrows his eyes. "You'll go now. It's dangerous out here, especially at night."

"The only thing dangerous out here is you, and I'm not afraid."

"You should be." Something besides anger flashes in his eyes, and it's enough to cause me to back up a step. He matches my step, moving toward me, forcing me to step backward again. "Go home, Kat, before I take you there myself."

I don't know if it's the fact that he won't back down or because I truly am tired from my run, but I decide to give in just this once. With a final glare, I turn away from the man I'll never understand and jog home.

TWENTY-ONE

What makes us most powerful can also kill us.

Rose's words haunt me for the rest of the week, especially after I've seen just how powerful our magic is, and I haven't even begun to scratch the surface.

Her words continued to shake me, all through my days as I studied Solstice law. At night, I would practice my magic with Charlotte and Rose. We've focused primarily on manipulation—creating, shaping, and combining elements to create things like wind blasts and shaped glass. Turns out, there's an entire science behind what my powers are capable of, hence the reason I agreed to attend the School of Gaia in the fall. To think I have all this power in my grasp is unnerving, to say the least. I'm going to need all the help I can get.

By the time Fourth of July comes around, jitters are sparking off my every nerve ending. While I'm excited to see Alec again, I'm more anxious than anything else.

"Be careful, Katrina," Rose warned.

I took her hand and looked her dead in the eyes. "I will.

What's the big deal, anyway? You like Alec. You were the one trying to set me up with him."

Rose sighed. "Yes, for selfish reasons, I'll admit. I just want you to be aware. Young love makes us foolish, and we can become distracted. It's a dangerous game to play, especially when your magic is new. You're vulnerable."

"Vulnerable, as in weak?"

She tugged on my hand, which was still holding hers, and squeezed. "I'm saying your magic is more powerful than you know what to do with. And that makes you a target."

"A target for who?"

I could tell she didn't want to speak the words aloud, but in the end, she gave me enough to chill my bones. "Erebus. He has been gone for a long time, but that doesn't mean he's gone for good. His Equinox Followers travel with him from community to community, then they walk among us, watch our every move, and report back to the God of Darkness when the time is right. Erebus will be back, and when that day comes, we'll need you at your strongest."

For a full evening, I considered missing the beach party, but when I woke up, I knew I couldn't disappoint Alec. I would go, and I would be careful.

I approach the party at just past seven, and it's like a scene from a movie. Boisterous voices spill across the beach. A growing bonfire sits near the shore. People are dancing merrily along the edge of the water. Farther up the beach, a volleyball game is in full swing. On the pool deck of Alec's house, a crowd has gathered around a Ping-Pong match, but most of the guests are below, where a band is playing on the terrace.

I finally spot Alec near the volleyball crowd and walk toward him.

"Hey, Kat," a voice calls.

My stomach twists when I recognize Iris's voice. Disappointed, I turn to find an over-exaggerated look of confusion on her face. "Hi, Iris. It's nice to see you again." I give her my friendliest greeting while pinching out my best smile.

"Can't say the same for you." Her sugary-sweet tone alerts all my senses. Her fake smile widens, and she tilts her head in what appears to be an effort to lay it on thick. "I'm surprised to see you here."

In the past, I would have cowered at the confrontation, but not this time. A wave of courage rips through me. I straighten and hold Iris's eyes in mine. "Alec invited me."

She narrows her eyes while still holding her smile.

"As his date," I add for good measure.

Iris loses ground slightly as she shrinks before me. "Please. Alec probably just feels sorry for you. He's nice to everyone. He can't help himself."

I roll my eyes and take a step to move around her. "Think what you want, Iris. I really don't care." But as soon as I take a step past her, her hand swings out and grips mine to stop me.

"Rumor was that you'd be long gone by now."

"Plans changed," I shoot back.

"Isn't that unfortunate?"

I notice her wandering eyes and unsteady stance, making it appear as if she's been drinking. I yank my arm from her grip, and that's when I catch a whiff of her next breath, confirming my suspicions. "I know what you're trying to do, but you don't intimidate me, Iris."

She narrows her eyes at me and takes a step forward. "Careful," she says while pointing a finger at me. "You don't know who you're messing with." She sways slightly.

I just shake my head. "I think you have it backward."

She doesn't retaliate like I expect. Instead, her eyes drop, and she almost falls backward. I'm quick to catch her, but she shoves me away.

"Don't touch me, you witch!"

She spits the words, and I reel back, wide-eyed, heart thumping with a quickening pace. Fear is the first emotion that comes to me. *What does she know?* Then another emotion creeps in as the blood beneath my skin comes to a boil. Anger. I'm not a witch. Not in the way she means it.

My insides begin to shake with fury, and my eyes narrow hard on her. The look she gives me now is one I will never forget. Terror. She stumbles and falls back, her butt hitting the sand while her eyes stare up at me as if I'm a monster. She starts to crawl backward, away from me, and I instinctively grab my necklace and squeeze it tightly. My next breath is a deep one, and on my exhale, I can feel all the wound-up parts of me start to relax.

"I told you to stop drinking!"

I'm shaken from the blackness when I hear Alec's voice. I look up to find him and Ava approaching. He walks up behind Iris, grips under her arms, and pulls her to her feet. As soon as she's standing, she begins to clutch her head as if she's suffering from a migraine.

Meanwhile, Ava is full of deep laughter. I just stare at

them both, taken aback by their behavior. Ava wraps an arm around Iris and pulls her away.

After they're far enough up the beach, Alec turns toward me. "I think they started drinking a little too early."

I turn away from their departing figures and frown, still shaken by Iris's behavior. "That was quite the welcome."

Alec cringes. "Sorry about that. Was she awful to you?"

I give him a sheepish smile and respond without actually answering. "Are you surprised?"

He lets out a sympathetic smile and reaches for my hand. "No. But for what it's worth, I'm glad you came." He tugs me forward and places his hands on my waist. There's a twinkle in his eyes. "You look nice."

Charlotte assured me the long orange maxi skirt and white crop tank top was the perfect outfit to wear to a beach party. I'm glad I listened. I look him up and down. He's wearing navy-and-white pinstriped swim shorts and a navy-blue muscle tank.

"You don't look so bad yourself." I can feel myself blush. "It looks like a great party."

"Yeah, well, some people are having too much fun." He directs his gaze where Ava and Iris walked off to. "But you made it."

I narrow my eyes at him. "I did, and now you owe me."

Alec leads me a short distance to the refreshment table, where a bowl of pink liquid sits in the center. He pours a drink and offers it to me. "A token of my gratitude." He bows dramatically.

"Funny," I say as I laugh. I look into the cup, checking out the drink.

As if he can read my mind, he laughs and says, "It's just punch." He gives me a boyish smile. "My parents and their friends are all over this joint. I couldn't get away with sneaking a single ounce of booze. Trust me."

"But Iris and Ava are getting it somewhere, right?"

Alec shrugs. "They probably brought it. My parents would never say anything to them, though. My parents intensely dislike their parents, so it's not worth the drama."

I laugh. "But you're still friends with them?"

Alec shrugs. "Keep your enemies close, right?" He winks.

"Well, then cheers," I say, a teasing tone in my voice as I raise my cup in the air.

"Cheers," he says. "To you for finally escaping from prison."

We tap our drinks together and take a sip, our eyes never leaving each other's.

"So, are you free from now on, or does your carriage turn back into a pumpkin at midnight?"

I smile and tilt my head. "I don't know about tonight, but we can start going running again if you want."

He grins. "I've been training, you know? You're not going to be able to blow me out of the water this time."

"Is that so?"

He nods, his confidence bolder than I remember. I think I like it too much.

"I'll accept that challenge."

He waggles his brows. "Now that we have that settled, come with me."

He whisks me away, past the volleyball game, through the throng of guests, and down to where a bunch of familiar people are lighting off fireworks. I remember a lot of them from our pool game at Island Grille. Brett gives me a quick wink and a wave. Trisha wraps me in an excited hug. And the rest of them offer friendly smiles that make me feel an overwhelming sense of happiness. It's like I might actually fit in with Alec and his friends—well, most of them. I sour at the thought of Iris and Ava, but the feeling fades quickly when Alec grabs a handful of sparklers and a lighter off a long table and motions for me to follow him closer to the water.

Alec lights the first sparkler, and it crackles to life. He hands it to me then lights one for himself. I wave my wand and watch as sparks shower from the stick and vanish into the night. I follow his lead and start to create random shapes. I barely notice that I'm using magic until I realize the heart I just made is lingering in the air longer than anything Alec is creating.

"Hey, Kat," Alec says, getting my attention. "What does this spell?"

I pay close attention to the words he's waving into the air, not missing a beat when I read, "Kiss me."

I must be blushing. My neck and cheeks feel warm, and I can't keep the smile off my face. "Smooth," I tease.

Alec takes my burnt-out sparkler from my hand and places mine and his in a bucket of water, then interlaces my fingers with his, he starts to run up the beach.

I laugh at his spontaneity. "Where are we going?"

"Somewhere away from here."

We find a quiet spot on top of a sand dune, farther back

from the party, where the noise becomes a faint background music to our perfect night.

"So, tell me, Summer Girl. How do you like it here? And be honest."

"I like it," I tell him without an ounce of hesitation. "I didn't think I would. And at first, I didn't." I laugh. "But this place—" I look across the water and smile. "It's grown on me. It almost feels like home."

The look he gives me next isn't a smile exactly, but I feel it deeply—like he's been holding his breath since the day I arrived, waiting for me to say I'll stay, then maybe I'll choose him. It's ridiculous, I know. My thoughts are just fantasies, obviously, because there's no way I can be feeling this strongly for a guy I barely know.

He squeezes my hand. "Then you must like living with Rose. I know you were unsure at first."

I nod. It was only a month ago, but it feels like it's been so much longer. "Turns out, she's pretty great."

"My parents seem to think so. I mean, she has helped Apollo Beach through a lot."

"A lot of what?" I'm so curious. Sometimes I think Rose downplays her legacy in this town.

"Well, apparently around two decades ago, there were a lot of violent crimes. Your grandparents led the effort to put an end to it all."

I make a mental note to ask Rose about that later, but the next few moments are silent. A gentle breeze blows between us as we stare out at the water. It's a beautiful night. The bay is calm, the stars are twinkling brightly upon us, and the thin crescent moon rests peacefully in the sky.

I start to absentmindedly imagine the sand in front of me twirling, and it begins to follow my thoughts. It's such a subtle movement that Alec doesn't notice. If he did, he would just think it was the wind. A hint of a smile plays on my face as I create a stronger breeze and swirl more sand into the tiny cyclone. The more I practice, the easier my powers become. It's intoxicating. As the wind grows more powerful, my creation grows into something that resembles a miniature tornado.

"Do you see that?" Alec squints and leans forward to get a closer look.

My heart jumps. I notice Alec react, and my heart races with panic. Charlotte's words come back to me. *The moment you begin to lose yourself in your magic, hold your necklace tightly. It will guide you back to calm. It's your best tool to keep you from using your magic beyond your limits.* I heed her warning and clutch my emerald in my palm. I close my eyes and will the wind to calm.

"That was strange," Alec says a second later.

My eyes open to find nothing but a crater of sand where the mini tornado was swirling moments ago. "What's that?"

"You didn't see that? A gust of wind created a small tornado right there in front of us." His expression is one of fascination, and he gets up to examine what was once my magical masterpiece.

If Rose finds out about this, she will be furious. I shrug. "I didn't see anything." I don't know what else to say. I've never been the best liar. My mom would always tell me she could see right through me. I try to think of how to change the subject. "Do you think Iris and Ava will ever warm up to me?"

Alec soon forgets about the sand and looks at me. "Probably not." He smiles then shrugs. "I had hope, but I've given up on that."

I make a noise in the back of my throat. "Well, that's just great. I didn't do anything to them."

Alec tilts his head. "No, but you have my attention in a way I've never given it to them."

I suck in a breath. "How is that?"

His gaze dips down to my lips. He inches closer, his fingers playing with a loose strand of my hair. "Maybe it's the way I look at you when I think no one else is watching." He leans in slightly. "Or maybe it's the way I can't help but smile when you're near." He leans in again so there's only an inch of space between our lips. "Maybe it's how I can have dozens of my friends together at a party and not give a damn because it's you who steals all my attention." His hand leaves my hair and makes its way to my neck until he's gently stroking it with his thumb.

My heart is going crazy, its erratic beat consuming all the space in my chest. As he starts to close the final gap between our lips, my heart feels like it's about to burst through my chest. I shut my eyes and completely give in to this new feeling of—I can't even think.

Everything feels so perfect. Fireworks are whizzing through the night sky, lighting it up like colored popcorn. Laughter and chatter fill the space around us. A crowd cheers in response to the end of the band's last song.

As soon as his lips touch mine, it feels like our first kiss all over again. He tastes of salt and fruit punch. I'm thankful we're sitting this time, because my knees turn to Jell-O. His lips firm against mine before the kiss deepens, his tongue sweeping the inside of my mouth. A rush shoots through me.

When our mouths separate and our faces draw apart a few seconds later, my lips are tingling. Our eyes meet, and smiles form on both our faces. He starts to lean in for more, but in the moment before we connect, something whizzes through the air and smacks hard into the side of my face. It makes a popping sound, and water bursts around me. I gasp and reach up to touch my stinging cheek. Looking down, I find a broken water balloon in my lap.

It doesn't take me long to guess where that came from, but I'm too shocked to move. I hear the adolescent giggles of Iris and Ava as they approach, then their annoying voices get louder.

"Oops. We're so sorry, Kat. We were just playing around." Iris's voice is high-pitched and riddled with fake sympathy.

I remain silent, anger bubbling inside me again. I grab my necklace, knowing I'll need all the help in the world to get my anger get under control.

I look over at Alec, who seems just as shocked. His shirt is damp, and he's looking at me like he's assessing the damage. His eyes sweep briefly over my soaked top. When his eyes turn toward Iris and Ava, he looks furious.

"It was just an accident," Iris says defensively, although she's still laughing.

"You two are behaving like assholes," he says, exasperated. "You should leave."

"Alec, c'mon. It was just an accident, and we apologized," Iris whines.

"We're not going anywhere." Ava says firmly. "We haven't even checked out the bonfire yet."

I'm so busy swiping my hands against my drenched outfit —I'm tempted to use my powers to dry it completely, but I resist—that I don't even notice when Iris and Ava walk off.

"I'll be right back," Alec says, his eyes on their departing figures. "I'm going to find them a ride home."

"Wait." I grab his wrist. "It was just a water balloon." I smile. "It's really not a big deal. Don't send them home. It will only cause a bigger scene and give them more reason to hate me."

He sighs and looks to be giving in.

I tug at his hand. "Walk with me to the water?"

Hesitating, he throws the girls a parting glance then takes my hand. We walk toward the water, sinking our feet sinking into the sand once we reach the edge. Fireworks are still exploding in the distance, but this time, there are thunderous pops and screams accompanying them. We both look toward the noise.

Iris and Ava are running around the bonfire, giggling.

"Are they holding fireworks?" I can't hold back from the horror that makes it into my voice.

"What the hell is wrong with them?" Alec says nothing else. It's all in his expression as he charges off toward the bonfire, where the girls are screaming and laughing hysterically. One of them trips and falls, but she gets back up again and continues to run.

When Alec catches up with them, things seem to settle

down, so I turn back toward the water. But almost as soon as I've turned around, I hear another outburst of screams. I turn back to the fire to see Alec, Ava, and Iris fighting. Their voices grow louder and louder.

"Go home," Alec roars. "You've been nothing but trouble all night."

Iris turns her dagger-like eyes on him. "It's a party, Alec. Lighten up."

"Someone is going to get hurt."

Iris steps closer to him and glares. "You're the one who's going to get hurt, hanging out with that Summer girl. I warned you about her, Alec. But you won't listen. She's a witch. Just like her grandmother." The disgust in Iris's voice is clear.

And there it is. That word. *Witch.* Fire builds up inside me.

"Because what you're saying is crazy," Alec says in my defense.

Iris continues to blast me with her hateful words, and Alec continues to defend me. I try to turn off their conversation, but I'm already bristling with anger. I can feel the temperature in my body rising higher and higher like a bubbling cauldron. This is new. Not euphoric like when I used my powers before. This is different. Strange. Angry.

Something in the sky pulls my focus. Dark, ominous clouds swarm in to cover the entire beach. I panic, knowing I need to find a way to calm down before I lose control completely.

Iris throws herself into Alec's arms and slams her mouth onto his to kiss him. Anger spirals inside of me. It's too much. My hands ball into tight fists, and before I know what's happening, a ball of energy explodes from my chest and hurtles straight toward the threesome.

My mouth grows wide in horror as I watch the scene unfold in slow motion. Iris reels back from my blast as she's propelled toward the bonfire.

TWENTY-TWO

Terror fills Alec's expression as he lunges for Iris and wraps his arms around her body. He yanks her back from the raging fire, and they crash onto the sand. Fire whooshes to life as if it's just been fueled with gas, then a thunderous growl shakes the sky overhead. Guests are already fleeing the hot, deafening flames, scattering in all directions.

Instinctively, I move toward the fire to help, although I don't know how. But the moment I try to take my first step, I realize just how far my feet have slipped beneath the surface. I try to yank them free, but I'm trapped, held prisoner by the grip of wet sand. With every wave that moves over the shore, I sink deeper. My new strength is no match for the force keeping me here. I give another tug of my leg to try to free one foot, but I lose my balance. Then a great force propels me forward, and I fall face-first onto the shore.

Screams, gasps, and cries burst from the crowd of guests, who are running in all directions. When I look back toward Alec and Iris, I see that the wind has taken control of the fire completely. I can't even see them anymore. The bonfire has nearly tripled in size, its wild flames the shape of arms, reaching outward as if trying to sweep anyone and anything into its deadly inferno.

I grab my necklace and close my eyes, my focus on the earth that shackles my legs and feet. "Release me!" I scream over the sound of the flames. Nothing immediately happens, but I'm not ready to give up. I can't just stand here. I need to help them.

"Release me now!" I scream again, more commanding this time, my voice reverberating with the wind. The sand loosens around me, giving me the burst of confidence I need. It's working—I look back at the orange billowing flames that are growing with every second—but not fast enough.

I use all my heightened strength to wrestle and claw my way out of the hole I've sunk into. I have to help Alec and Iris. I search for them again and gasp when a figure emerges from the flames. It's Iris. I recognize her blond hair first, though half of it glows like hot embers, as if it's about to ignite any second. I fear that's exactly what it's about to do.

Alec is there, pulling her a safe distance from the fire. He doesn't see the gust of wind that sweeps the flames toward them as it doubles again in size and takes up nearly half of the beach.

"Run!" I scream.

Alec looks over his shoulder, his eyes spreading wide. He pulls Iris to her feet, but she's too limp to stand on her own. He throws her over his shoulder and starts to run, but the flames act like magnets, threatening to catch them if they slow at all. I hear Alec scream out for Ava to run. She's just standing off to the side, appearing frozen with shock. The horror of the scene before her is written all over her face.

Adrenaline surges through me. "Release me now!" I scream it one last time, and it's finally enough. I yank my foot to release myself from the sand. I'm back on the shore, ready to take off toward the fire. There's got to be a way I can put it out. But before I make it far, a wave of smoke blows toward me, encasing me like a shield. I turn in a circle. The cloud thickens into a black wall, and it's closing in on me.

As it nears my face, I begin to gasp then choke. I fall back, feeling defeated. How do I stop the fire? I think hard, trying to recall anything that I've practiced that can help.

That's it. Water. I look up at the dark clouds overhead and decide to use them to my advantage. I raise my hands, palms toward the clouds, and use all my energy, everything I possess, to call the rain from the sky. When the first drop lands on my nose, I know it's working, but a light drizzle isn't going to stop that fire.

I use my hand to clear the wall of smoke, but panic surges through me when I see the fire still raging on. *I need more water.* I look over my shoulder toward the bay's now-restless surface. I don't even know if this is something I'm capable of, but I know I need to try.

I face the water and let my inner strength guide me. Slowly, I raise my arms toward the waves rolling in toward the beach, then focus as hard as I've ever had to do. Something deep inside me vibrates, like my core is the root of my power and it's bracing itself for war. A force radiates through me and blasts through my fingertips, commanding the water to operate at my will. Then it happens.

There's a wave growing in the distance, gaining height as it gets close, until it's like a tsunami, towering over the shore. With a final command, I bring the wave toward me, toward the threatening fire, knowing there's nowhere for me to go except through it.

When the gargantuan wall of water is standing nearly an inch before me, I squeeze my eyes shut and drop my arms, giving the surge free rein to stamp out the fire once and for all. I only have time for a short breath before it crashes over me.

For what seems like an eternity, its deep currents throw me around like a rag doll. I use all my strength and held breath to claw my way toward the surface. I don't know how far I need to rise, so I just keep on swimming, but I'm continuously dragged back down and am rapidly using up my held breath.

Breath is rapidly leaving my lungs now, and I grow weaker until darkness begins to take over my sight. My energy is depleted. My chances of holding on are slimming to zero. So I do the only thing I can think of and release my will and float freely within the lulling quiet of the water until an eerie peace fills my dreamlike state.

What makes us most powerful can also kill us.

I imagine Rose talking to me now, her stark warnings making complete sense. I should have listened. I should never have gone to the party. There is obviously so much I don't know about myself or my powers—and clearly, there are things I cannot control.

I grab hold of my emerald. My last hope. I attempt to squeeze it tightly, but my strength is gone, my power drained. Feeling utterly lifeless, I float away into my own consuming darkness.

Not even my magic can save me now.

TWENTY-THREE

I'm starting to see things.

A shiny blue fin passes by me. I recognize it from my dream. Only this time, I see more of it. The V-shaped fin is a beautiful iridescent sort of blue, sparkling when it catches a glint of light from the moon. It's attached to a long tail, narrow at the bottom and curving in until it meets the body of the most beautiful girl I've ever seen. She has long red hair, a creamy complexion, and sparkling green eyes.

I'm mesmerized by her beauty. As she swims closer, her hypnotic eyes hold mine, nulling all my thoughts of death. Then she scoops me into her strong arms and carries me up where the water meets the air. Maybe there's hope for me yet.

We're nearing the surface of the water when a strange black shadow covers the light from the moon. The girl's arms slip away, and no matter how desperate I am for that small taste of air, I'm sinking beneath another wave.

My lungs burn. My muscles are weak, and just as I give up all hope, arms dip into the water above me and yank me to the surface. I scream, causing water to bubble around me as I use the last of the air in my lungs.

Strong arms tighten around my waist and pull me to the water's surface. I've swallowed so much liquid, it feels as though I'm still drowning, but the gentle breeze and the sound of waves crashing around me tell me I'm being lifted into the air.

As I fade in and out of consciousness, the rest seems to happen so fast.

I'm laid on a cold, hard surface.

The floor beneath me is rocking with the waves.

Hands push hard against the center of my chest.

I'm struggling to breathe, but it still feels like I'm drowning.

A mouth lands on mine...

Pressure flows into my lungs, causing water to gush from my mouth. Water continues to empty from my stomach, and I can finally breathe again. I gasp for air as if it's my last breath.

There's a tightening on my wrist, and something snaps...

Then darkness finds me again.

"KAT, WAKE UP," a voice pleads over and over until I'm pulled from my darkness.

I look up and find Alec, his wondrous green eyes shining down on me.

"Kat." He's relieved. He looks tired and scared, like he thought I was dead.

I try to sit up. I want him to know I'm okay, but I quickly become dizzy and I fall back again. My head hits the sand. *Sand? Wait. I thought I was on a boat.* Before that, everything is foggy.

"Just relax, okay? You almost drowned." Alec's concern strengthens me.

But I did drown, I want to say. *Someone pulled me out of the water.* Then I remember Iris.

"The fire! Alec, is Iris okay?"

"She'll be okay, but she's badly burned, really shaken up, and in a lot of pain. The ambulance is coming."

As if on cue, a siren blares in the distance. I pull myself to a sitting position to take a look around. The crowd has thinned significantly, and the remaining guests huddle in clusters, while watching the aftermath of the freak fire and windstorm that terrorized the entire party.

Alec looks worriedly at me and wraps me in a hug. "Are you okay?" The concern in his voice tugs at my heart, but I'm too disturbed from the events to return his affection.

I find the strength to nod. "I'm okay."

Apparently, the croak in my voice tells him differently because he looks down at me with a helpless expression. He shakes his head, unbelieving. "That wave almost killed you, and it saved Iris's life." There's a clear look of bewilderment in his expression. "I don't even know how that was possible. We don't get waves like that here."

Guilt shakes through me to the point where I become nauseated at the knowledge that everything that happened tonight, including my near-death accident, was completely in my control. Or it should have been. But like Rose warned, I wasn't ready.

I look over where Iris lies. Her hair is gone, her scalp is covered with blood, and a tear rolls down her cheek. She moans with pain, and my heart breaks for her. She was drunk, reckless, and mean, but she didn't deserve what my magic did to her. I caused this. Maybe I should have died under that wave, but someone pulled me out of the water. But who?

"How did I get back on the beach? I got caught in a wave that took me under. I was drowning, and someone pulled me out."

Alec shakes his head. "I don't know. I saw you go under, and you were gone for a long time. Then, I don't know how, but you just washed up on shore. I didn't see anyone else."

I shiver then look at the sky. Closing my eyes, I soak in the light of the moon, hoping I can reenergize so I can help Iris. When I feel my energy begin to rebuild, I clamber to my feet and go to Iris's side. I place one hand on my emerald and the other over her heart. But something feels wrong.

My bracelet. The emerald is still secured around my neck, but the charm bracelet and locket my mom gave me are gone. *No.* My heart thuds deeply in my chest. My breath is caught in my throat, and I struggle to take another breath as panic sets in. *How could I have lost my mother's locket?* A tear falls down my cheek, and I want to sob, but I need to help Iris.

Alec was right. Iris's injuries are almost too much to stomach. I can't completely see her scalp through the blood, but there's no doubt that she's been badly burned.

"Katrina." Rose's shrill voice startles me. "What happened?"

I release my necklace and stare up at my grandmother and Charlotte. I open my mouth to speak, but Alec cuts in. "The bonfire got out of control." I hadn't even seen him approach.

Rose's gaze moves from Alec to me then stays on me. I know there will be consequences for what I did tonight, but I'm not ready to face them right now. Not until Iris is okay.

"Hey, someone should probably meet the ambulance on the street so they know where we are." It's the first thing I can think of to make him go away. If I'm going to heal Iris, then he can't be here.

"Good idea," Alec says. "I'll be back."

As soon as he's far enough away, I lean in closer to Iris and clutch my emerald again. My stomach churns at the sight of her burns. Fortunately, the fire didn't spread farther than that.

Rose and Charlotte shift so they are on the other side of her body. I'm glad they are here to help.

Iris opens her eyes, and tears flood her eyes. "It hurts, Kat."

My chest aches. "Shh, it's okay." I squeeze her hand. "You're going to be okay. Close your eyes."

Iris obeys, and I place my fingers on top of her head. I let the energy take over my body as I look to the moon for support, just as Rose and Charlotte taught me. I feel it—the tingling sensation in my fingers as it transfers to Iris and heals her wounds. I can even hear the energy sizzling in the air now that I'm focused on healing Iris and that alone.

Rose and Charlotte extend their hands, too, their power now an extension of mine. I look at them both as they pour their healing into Iris. *I've failed them.* But when Iris finally begins to relax, it's hard for me to be anything other than overwhelmingly relieved. Her eyes remain closed, and I think she's sleeping. Her heartbeat is strong. *She's going to be okay.*

Alec returns, directing the ambulance to pull onto the beach. I stand to greet him. "You should go with her."

Alec frowns. "What about you? You were hurt too, Kat." His voice is so gentle it sends a knife through my chest. He has no idea I caused this disaster. *He thinks I'm a victim.*

"We'll take care of Katrina," Rose says to him, her tone firm.

I give Alec a small smile. "I'll be okay, but Iris needs someone. You'll call her parents?"

"Already did. They're heading to the hospital now." Alec looks at me, defeated. "Kat, I don't want to leave you."

I reach for his hand and squeeze it. If he had any idea what I did tonight, he wouldn't want to be anywhere near me. My heart aches. He would hate me for what I am, for what I did. Still, I press my lips to his, not caring that Rose and Charlotte are standing by. "Go," I whisper.

After another second of hesitation, Alec jogs to the ambulance where the paramedics are placing Iris into the back of the van, and joins them.

I watch until the doors of the ambulance close behind him and the vehicle rolls away into the distance. With a final glance at the scene on the beach, I follow Rose and Charlotte back to Summer Manor—ready to face my fate.

TWENTY-FOUR

Back at Summer Manor, Rose and I sit facing each other in the great room. Charlotte has gone to make tea. Rose isn't looking at or speaking to me. Deep concentration is evident in her features. My heartbeat escalates as I replay the last couple of hours over and over in my mind, like a broken record. *What have I done? What will my punishment be?*

I look at Rose, considering the fact that she is disappointed in me. A sinking in my chest tells me I don't want that. Charlotte enters the room moments later with a tray and three full cups of tea. Steam rises from them, reminding me of the smoke from the billowing flames of the bonfire. I shudder.

"I felt trapped," I say, looking between them. "I didn't mean to push Iris into the flames, or to make the wind fuel the fire. And the wave—" I choke on my words. "I didn't mean for it to drown me." I bow my head. "I lost control, just like you said I would."

Neither of them says a word and that make me feel worse.

A million thoughts race through my mind, but one stands prominently there. I've read the Solstice law book from front to back, and one thing is abundantly clear. Those who abuse their powers will be punished. Rose has echoed those same words often. So now what? "Am I going to be punished for what I did?" My voice is weak, scared of whatever consequences I face.

Rose looks at me, her brows bent as a look of confusion appears on her face. "Punished for what, dear?"

Every thought I've had recently is halted by her words. Rose doesn't think I should be punished?

"Didn't you hear me? I caused all of this. I was angry. The wind got out of control and took the fire with it. I couldn't stop it. I tried, but I couldn't control my own powers. The law book says that punishment is worse than death."

Charlotte places a hand on my leg. "Kat, listen to what you're saying. You couldn't calm the fire because you weren't the one controlling it. The same goes for the wind."

My thoughts slow to a canter. "I don't understand."

Rose narrows her eyes at me, halting me in mid-breath. "You pushed that poor girl toward the fire, which you shouldn't have done, but someone else caused the fire to get out of control."

Again, I replay the events in my head. Only this time, I keep the law book in mind. "I can only control the powers I create." Although I should be elated at my relief, I'm struck now with a flood of new questions. "Then who? Who would want the fire to get so out of control? I swear that thing had arms and legs, and it was reaching for Alec and Iris."

Rose and Charlotte look at each other, fear evident in

their eyes. It's as if they are deciding who should deliver the news. "Kat," Rose stars slowly. "Do you remember the stories of Astina Summer and her evil counterpart? The enemy and his army that still exists today?"

I don't have to think too hard to remember her story vividly. "Yes. The God of Darkness, right?" Something clicks. "You're saying he was at the bonfire?"

Rose nods carefully. "Yes. And if Erebus is here, that means his Followers are here also. Erebus doesn't travel alone. He's too much of a coward. He forms groups where he travels, and he teaches them to hunt, taunt, and kill. Erebus hides behind his Followers. They do his bidding, but if they get caught or killed in the process, he can just walk away. He cares for no one."

It all feels like too much to process. "Maybe it wasn't him," I say, desperate to believe history isn't repeating itself. "Maybe it was all just a coincidence. There were fireworks near the fire, and—"

"We found his mark tonight, Katrina."

"His what?" My heart is beating so hard and fast, I need to focus to hear what she says next.

"Erebus leaves a mark in the wake of his destruction. A signature of sorts. An Enchanter who was there tonight found it carved into a log from the fire and brought it to us."

"What?" A shiver races down my spine.

Rose pauses for a moment, like she needs time to process all of this too. "It's a warning. He wants us to know he's watching. Erebus isn't an impulsive nemesis. He's calculated, manipulative, and clever. Tonight was only the beginning."

"The beginning of what exactly?"

Rose shakes her head. "I wish I knew."

I let out an exasperated breath. "What do you think he wants this time?"

"What he's always wanted. Power. Our community has only grown over the years, despite his threats. There's more for him to gain by killing us, but we've also made it much harder for him to do so. One of your grandfather's biggest legacies was using magic to protect certain areas of Apollo Beach to act as a safe haven for Enchanters. Erebus can't step foot on Summer Island or in an Enchanter's home, for instance."

I think about what happened on the beach tonight and frown. "Why didn't he protect all of Apollo Beach?"

"It's not that simple, dear. That form of magic is... complicated, to say the least."

Like during every conversation with Rose, I'm frustrated. She's so careful to not give out more information than a person can handle, but right now, I just want to know all of it. "What about his Followers? Are we protected from them too?"

Rose searches my eyes like she wants to tell me something but changes her mind. "Astina stripped them of their magic when she saw what Erebus was commanding of them. Erebus still employs his Equinox army to carry out evil acts. And they only have powers like ours when he possesses them."

I shudder. "He possesses them? As in takes over their body and controls their every move?"

Rose nods. "Precisely."

"But why hurt innocent people like Iris?"

"He can't fight us unless he makes us vulnerable first. So he causes harm to innocent people, then his army looks for those who do as an Enchanter would." Her eyes pierce mine and I'm taken back to Rose, Charlotte, and me on the beach, healing Iris.

"The fire was a trap?" My heartbeat quickens. "I created that wave. Do you think he knows about me?" My voice is shaky and full of emotion because I already know the answer to my question.

"You need not worry, Katrina. Erebus cannot harm you. There's a reason your mother gave you that bracelet. It protects you from Erebus. It..." Her voice trails off as her gaze drops to my wrist. She gasps, her shocked eyes rising to mine.

I clutch my bare wrist, and an overwhelming sense of loss fills me yet again. "I know. I must have lost it in the ocean." Tears blur my vision. "What do you mean it protects me from Erebus?"

Rose shakes her head like she refuses to say whatever it is on her mind. "It doesn't make sense," she whispers to herself.

"What doesn't make sense?" I rise to my feet, my anger blossoming rapidly.

When Rose looks back at me, I can tell she's trying to maintain a calm appearance, but whatever the loss of my bracelet means to her is making it impossible. "It doesn't make sense because without that bracelet, you're vulnerable to Erebus."

"Vulnerable how?" I demand.

Rose stands, her movements slow, her eyes set firmly on

mine. "You said you almost drowned under that wave. Your energy was depleted. Is that right?"

I nod, shuddering at the memory.

"Without that pendant, you wouldn't have had a chance against Erebus. He could have ended your life tonight, Katrina."

"Then why didn't he?"

In true Rose fashion, she pauses dramatically before speaking. "I don't know, but I have a feeling we're all about to find out."

THANK you so much for reading *Cursed*, Book One in the *Enchanted Gods Trilogy*. I hope you loved it. Fated releases on August 17th. Get ready for more romance, mystery, and twists you'll never see coming!

Keep reading for a sneak peek at FATED, Book Two! You can also...

PREORDER FATED
PREORDER TAKEN
ADD FATED TO GOODREADS
ADD TAKEN TO GOODREADS

Steam Level Warning: This series does get steamier with each book.

FATED PROLOGUE
COMING AUGUST 17TH

I didn't ask for this life. To finally have the one thing in this world worth living for then be forced to give it up is unbearable. He stands before me, yet out of my grasp. Now, he is forbidden to me, a temptation above any red fruit.

A pained look flickers across his expression, like I've hurt him, but he hurt me too. The knowledge of what he did is far more powerful than the tears that threaten to surface. I must will them away. To reveal my own pain would only complicate things. One thing, I know for sure—this is how things are destined to be.

Forcing my eyes away from his is my only hope at this moment. His heated stare stays on me. I can feel it burning a hole straight through my core.

How did it happen that the one I'm fated to love would turn out to be the one I need to kill to survive?

Keep reading for the first chapter of FATED or

PREORDER FATED
PREORDER TAKEN
ADD FATED TO GOODREADS
ADD TAKEN TO GOODREADS

Steam Level Warning: This series does get steamier with each book.

FATED CHAPTER 1
COMING AUGUST 17TH

Breeze from the bay whips my ponytail around as the freed tendrils of long brown hair smack my cheek. I tighten my grasp around the handlebars of my beach cruiser and place my right foot firmly on the concrete. As cars exit the one-lane bridge that leads to Summer Island, I smile easily at the drivers turning onto the main road.

There's something mystical about the ivy growing on the gate's concrete walls and the tall, dark kudzu-covered trees surrounding the entrance. *Mystical.* The single word seems to accurately describe my entire life-changing existence since moving to Apollo Beach. Who would have thought the teen who found trouble everywhere she turned wasn't cursed, but instead Enchanted?

A man in uniform steps outside the guard house building to wave. "Morning, Kat."

"Hey, Herkle." I recognized him instantly from my first few visits to the island. "Nice to see you again."

Herkle, Herkie, and Herk are all short for Hercules, from whom he descended. I put two and two together, and Charlotte confirmed it for me during dinner one night this past week. He's one of *us*—an Enchanter, a descendant of the gods from ancient Greece. It's still mind-boggling to know it's all real and this is my new life.

"I heard you had quite the Enchanting." His jovial smile is infectious.

I find myself smiling too. "It was definitely eye-opening, to say the least.

He chuckles. "We've all been there. Will I see you at the Enchanters' event tonight?"

I give him a knowing look. "Are you kidding? Charlotte is making me a dress for the occasion and everything. I'll be there."

Traffic clears, and I give Herkle a goodbye wave. I push to start pedaling again and take off down the long, winding tree-covered drive. It's been almost two months since I moved here, and I'm back on the job hunt. After my failed audition to waitress at Island Grille, I've decided to tempt fate and ask for another shot. It's not like I qualify for much. A job at the Apollo Beach Library would be another option, but after being holed up at Summer Manor for two weeks straight while doing nothing but reading the Solstice Law Book, I'm aiming for something—dare I say—fun.

I pedal faster to round the final curve before I get to the quaint village, which is reminiscent of ancient Greek landmarks and ruins. I'm nearly around the bend when a squirrel jumps out of the bushes and darts across the street just as a white van barrels around the corner.

"No," I gasp. With a quick turn of my bike, I pull out in front of the van and stick my foot out to stop my bike completely.

Tires squeal and swerve as the van attempts to break, but it's still going too fast. My pulse zooms through my veins as I think quickly. My new magic travels faster when I use my hands to propel it, but Charlotte has been teaching me how to exercise energy without having to be so obvious about it. This moment would be the appropriate time to try it.

I squeeze my eyes shut and clutch the handlebars of my bike before aiming all the energy I can muster toward the van. I can feel the explosion of energy burst from my pores. There's a loud crunching of metal, like the van just collided with a wall, and I look to see the squirrel dart into the bushes on the other side of the road.

With a quick sigh of relief, I look back toward the van. Its front grill is bent in the center and steam rises from around the hood. *Crap.* My eyes widen, and I release the handlebars of my bike, letting it fall to the ground beneath me.

The driver's door to the van bursts open, and cold-faced Johnny Pierce steps out. He slams the door behind him, his startling blue eyes narrowed on mine. "Are you kidding me with this? What the hell is your problem, Kat?"

An unexpected thrill races though me when Johnny says my name. I wasn't sure if we'd ever speak again after our run-in over a week ago. He was so cold. So angry. And now, he's a stark reminder of the very reason I should look for another job. It shouldn't be hard to find something else. But something about Island Grille calls to me. Or maybe I want to show Johnny he can't push me around.

"Earth to Kat. I asked you why you pulled out in front of me like a fucking lunatic."

I suck in a deep breath and instinctively reach for the energy stone I wear around my neck. It's supposed to calm me, but when it comes to Johnny, I'm not sure anything can calm me. "You were going too fast. Didn't you see the squirrel? You would have ran right over it."

Johnny's jaw tenses. "No, I didn't, because I was too focused on not hitting *you*. Didn't your granny tell you to pay attention and not to swerve in and out of traffic? This is practically a one-lane road. You should be more careful."

I let out a laugh and shrug. "I think I'll be just fine, but thanks for the advice. And you don't have to call her my 'granny,' like some condescending asshole. Her name is Rose."

"Just be careful next time," he growls. "I don't want to be responsible for killing some kid who can't pay attention to simple things like road signs."

"I'm eighteen."

"Yeah, well that's young enough."

I squint at him, trying to remember what he told me his age was. I swear he said it was twenty-two. "You're not much older than me." If it weren't for the stubble covering his mouth and cheeks, I would think we were the same age.

With an amused shake of my head, I lean over to pick up my bike and freeze when his hand brushes mine. Energy surges through my veins—I feel its buzz reverberate through me like it's lifting me high above the clouds—a strange sensation to have for someone I want to despise. Johnny grips the center bar of the bike and picks it up like it weighs nothing before popping it right-side-up on the drive.

"Are you okay to ride?"

His question throws me a little. It almost sounds like he cares, even though his reaction was delayed. "I'm fine. But why are you suddenly pretending to care?"

He shakes his head. "Trust me, I don't. Just trying to avoid a lawsuit." Still looking at me, he points to his van. "I already need to break it to the boss that I'm out of a catering van until we can get this one fixed."

I tilt my head and point to the van. "What for? It looks fine."

Johnny scrunches his face in confusion. "Huh? No, it's—" He's midturn when he spots the front of his van, which is now undamaged. He looks back at me. "I thought—"

I look at him with wide, innocent eyes. I might have repaired it when he wasn't looking. "You thought what?"

He shakes his head and takes a step back. "Nothing. It's all good." He makes it all the way to his van then swivels around. "You sure you don't need a ride somewhere? I'm not asking to be nice. I just have some time before my next event."

My heart kicks in my chest at the second semi-kind reaction he's had during our encounter. "No, I'm—" I start to tell him I'm going to Island Grille to beg Roy for a second chance, but I think better of it. If I tell Johnny that, his knee-jerk asshole tendencies might find a way to stop me. "Just heading to the library."

He makes a face to tell me I'm weirder than he initially thought, then he swings open his door, jumps inside, and starts the engine. I'm already riding off when I hear the van start up then drive away.

Using my strength, I pedal as fast as my legs will carry me in a desperate need to release the pent-up energy that my encounters with Johnny Pierce seem to create. He's impossible, but I'm not going to let him get to me the way I did before.

As I clear the winding drive and enter the main road that circles the island, I take in the small businesses, school, and government buildings that spread over the land. Everything one might want to experience exists here. It's no wonder the residents of the entire town of Apollo Beach can be found here on summer days like today.

A recreational spread sits at the center of the island, with basketball courts, a football field, a track, tennis courts, and four baseball diamonds. An oversized waterfall cascades into a narrow lazy river that winds around a hidden alcove then empties into a large beachfront pool.

I do a double take when I see the lifeguard at the main pool. He's perched high above the water, wearing long orange swim trunks, a whistle dangling from his neck.

Alec. There's a flip-flop sensation in my chest when I recognize him. As he rolls his neck, his messy auburn hair glistens in the sun. His chest muscles move slightly, catching a partial ray of light. Even though his eyes are hidden behind sunglasses, I would recognize him from a mile away.

Just thinking about the last time I saw him makes my throat tighten. A week has passed since the fateful night that almost killed Iris and me. The flames of the bonfire still blaze through my mind daily, and my near drowning haunts my nights before I drift off to sleep. Luckily, my nightmares have ended. The green emerald necklace protects my mind from the unpleasant dreams I was prone to prior to my Enchanting.

Evading Alec over the week has been like trying to pull a rock from cement, but there was no way I could face him until I came to grips with all the new information I learned after that night. I needed to focus on my new responsibility as a Solstice. I would never hurt Alec intentionally, but after seeing firsthand what my powers can and cannot do, I'm more afraid of what I cannot control—*Erebus and his Equinox Followers*. I couldn't afford to put anyone else in danger. So I made up excuse after excuse to distance myself for awhile—until Alec stopped calling.

Guilt pulses through my veins, but I shake it away and cycle off toward my destination. I park in front of Island Grille and take the steps two at a time. Trisha is at the podium at the entrance, with her head down, doodling on a dry-erase board. She must hear me coming, because her head snaps up.

Her eyes grow wide at the sight of me. "Kat, hi. Where have you been? Alec said he's tried calling."

I smile, happy to see her too. "I've just been laying low after everything went down, but I'm here now." With my hands on my hips, I tilt at my waist in a playful pose.

"Well, perfect timing, because we're all hanging out tomorrow for Alec's birthday."

A pang hits my chest. "It's his birthday tomorrow?" I had no idea.

"Yup, but after what happened on the Fourth, he doesn't

want to make a big deal about it. We don't have any concrete plans yet, but you're invited, and I'm pretty sure you owe us all for disappearing."

I let out an uncomfortable laugh. "I probably do owe you, but I don't know, Trisha. Who else will be there?"

"Alec, Brett, me, and—" She cringes, and it makes my stomach churn. "Ava, but she's different now that Iris is pretty much grounded for life. She's less... Ava."

Laughing, I shake my head. "Let me get back to you on that."

Trisha sighs, but relents, then she tilts her head. "What are you doing here? Grabbing some breakfast?"

I let my eyes dart around in an attempt to spot the owner. "Yeah, I was hoping to speak with Roy and see if he's willing to give me another shot. I just don't think there's another job on the island I want."

"Oh," Trisha says with a shrug. "Well, that's easy. Roy put me in charge of hiring for the summer since he'll be so busy and Johnny can be so unpleasant. Roy doesn't want to deal with it. So—" She grins and reaches out her hand. "Welcome to the team. You start in two days."

I take her hand, and we shake, a cheesy grin lifting my cheeks. "And here I was, terrified to come back by. If this didn't work out, I was going to try the marina."

Trisha gives a vigorous shake of her head. "Don't you dare work at that creepy marina. It's beautiful during the day, but I wouldn't want to go anywhere near that place at night. You'll fit in just fine here. And it's not Roy you need to be terrified of."

I pout, already knowing what she's going to say, then we say the words together, "It's Johnny."

Make sure to...

PREORDER FATED
PREORDER TAKEN
ADD FATED TO GOODREADS
ADD TAKEN TO GOODREADS

Steam Level Warning: This series does get steamier with each book.

LET'S CONNECT

Want to stay updated with the latest news by connecting with me on social media and signing up for my mail list. You'll never miss a new release, event, or sale!

Subscribe for Updates: www.smarturl.it/KK_MailList
TikTok: www.tiktok.com/@k.k.allen
Instagram: www.Instagram.com/KKAllen_Author
Facebook: www.Facebook.com/AuthorKKAllen
Goodreads: www.goodreads.com/KKAllen
BookBub: www.bookbub.com/profile/k-k-allen
Website: www.KKAllen.com

Join Forever Young!

Enjoy special sneak peeks, participate in exclusive giveaways, enter to win ARCs, and chat it up with K.K. and special guests ;)

www.facebook.com/groups/foreveryoungwithkk

ACKNOWLEDGMENTS

Writing Cursed has been an absolute dream come true and I could not have done it without the folks I'm about to mention!

To my Beta Babes—Cyndi, Sammie, Renee, Patricia, Emily, and Suzanne. Thank you for bringing your brutal honesty, your excitement, and your dedication to these stories. I couldn't have done this without you.

To Lindsey and Renee, the badass ladies who are with me behind the scenes daily, always making sure I'm not getting lost in my own thoughts, I can't imagine a day when one of you isn't telling me what to do. I live for it. Haha.

To Harloe and Heather, our friendship means everything to me. Thank you for always being there during the highs and lows and in between. I'm so ready for our epic reunion.

A huge shoutout to my cover designer for the *Enchanted Gods* series, Emily Wittig. You captured this world perfectly!

Thank you to Dani at Wildfire for being the absolute best from the very beginning. I love working with you!

To Tasha, my real life Trisha. Love you to pieces.

To my family who inspires me every day—Jagger, for

being the best son I could ever ask for. Your imagination is your key to this life, babe. Never lose that Enchanter spirit. T, for telling me to publish my very first book, and for so much more. Mom, for being my first reader ever and showing up in various ways in my novels. Dad and Ed, for bringing my father figures to life in my stories. Corey and Brandon—for being brothers who I don't see nearly enough, but I'm so proud of both of you. Love you all so much.

To all the bloggers who stepped up to try something new from a contemporary romance author! Thank you for trusting me. I hope you loved it. I can't wait for you to read more.

To my Angsters, Forevers, and Booksters. Without you, I'd be lost!

Last but not least, to my readers. I'm so grateful you took a chance on me. I cannot wait for you to read *Fated*!

Much love and HEAs,
K.K. Allen

OTHER NOVELS

Up in the Treehouse

Haunted by the past, Chloe and Gavin are forced to come to terms with all that has transpired to find the peace they deserve. Except they can't seem to get near each other without combatting an intense emotional connection that brings them right back to where it all started . . . their childhood treehouse.

Under the Bleachers

Fun and flirty Monica Stevens lives for food, fashion, and boys ... in that order. The last thing she wants to take seriously is dating. When a night of flirty banter with Seattle's hottest NFL quarterback turns passionate, her care-free life could be at risk.

Through the Lens

When Maggie moves to Seattle for a fresh start, she's presented with an unavoidable obstacle—namely, the cocky chef with a talent for photography and getting under her skin. Can they learn to get along for the sake of the ones they love?

Over the Moon

Silver Livingston has spent the past eight years hiding from her past when the NFL God, Kingston Scott, steps off the bus to mentor a football camp for kids. Kingston wants to be anywhere but at Camp Dakota...until he sees her. The intoxicating woman with the silver moon eyes, the reserved smile, and the past she's determined to keep hidden.

Dangerous Hearts (A Stolen Melody, #1)

Lyric Cassidy knows a thing or two about bad boy rock stars with raspy vocals. In fact, her heart was just played by one. So when she takes an assignment as road manager for the world famous rock star, Wolf, she's prepared to take him on, full suit of heart-armor intact.

Destined Hearts (A Stolen Melody, #2)

But with stolen dreams, betrayals, and terrifying threats--no one's heart is safe. Not even the ones that may be destined to be together.

British Bachelor

Runaway British Bachelor contestant, Liam Colborn, is on the run from the press. When he gets to Providence, RI to stay with his late brother's best friend, all he wants is a little time to regroup from his time on a failed reality show. That is, until he meets the redheaded bombshell nanny who lives in the pool house.

Waterfall Effect

Lost in the shadows of a tragedy that stripped Aurora of everything she once loved, she's back in the small town of Balsam Grove, ready to face all she's kept locked away for seven years. Or so she thinks.

A Bridge Between Us

With a century-old feud between neighboring families with only a bridge to separate them, Camila and Ridge find themselves wanting to rewrite the future. It all starts with an innocent friendship and quickly builds to so much more in this second chance coming of age romance.

Center of Gravity (Gravity, #1)

She was athleticism and grace, precision and passion, and she had a stage presence he couldn't tear my eyes from. He wanted her...on his team, in his bed. There was only one problem... He couldn't have both.

Falling From Gravity (Gravity, #1.5)

If I hadn't considered Amelia dangerous before, I certainly did now. She wasn't anything like I had expected. Even after all these years—of living so close to her, of listening to her giggle with my sister in the bedroom next to mine—I hadn't given much thought to my sister's best friend.

Defying Gravity (Gravity, #2)

The ball is her Amelia's court, but Tobias isn't below stealing--her power, her resolve, her heart... When he wants a second chance to reignite our connection, the answer is simple. They can't. Not unless they defy the rules their dreams were built on and risk everything.

The Trouble With Gravity (Gravity #3)

When Sebastian makes Kai an offer she can't afford to refuse, she learns signing on will mean facing the tragedy she's worked so hard to shut out. He says she can trust him to keep her safe, but is her heart safe too?

ABOUT THE AUTHOR

K.K. Allen is a *USA Today* bestselling and award-winning author who writes heartfelt and inspirational contemporary romance stories. K.K. is a native Hawaiian who graduated from the University of Washington with an Interdisciplinary Arts and Sciences degree and currently resides in central Florida with her ridiculously handsome little dude who owns her heart.

K.K.'s publishing journey began in June 2014 with a young adult contemporary fantasy trilogy. In 2016, she published her first contemporary romance, *Up in the Treehouse*, which went on to win the Romantic Times 2016 Reviewers' Choice Award for Best New Adult Book of the Year.

With K.K.'s love for inspirational and coming of age stories involving heartfelt narratives and honest emotions, you can be assured to always be surprised by what K.K. releases next.

Made in the USA
Columbia, SC
03 August 2021

42587582R00157